THE BARGHEST

A MIDNIGHT GUNN NOVEL #2

C. L. MONAGHAN

The Barghest
A Midnight Gunn Novel #2
Copyright © 2020 Claire Monaghan
Published by Hudson Indie Ink
www.hudsonindieink.com

The Barghest/C.L. Monaghan – 2nd ed.
ISBN-13 - 978-1-913904-07-4

For my husband

PROLOGUE

KING'S CROSS, MAY 1862

The sound of the train's whistle prompted the straggling passengers to embark in a flurry of movement. Miss Agnes Carmichael hastily fished out the letter from her new black leather purse and shoved it into Giles Morgan's gloved hand.

"Please post this for me, Mr. Morgan. It's for my father."

"Of course, Miss Carmichael," he replied, carefully inserting the letter into his inside coat pocket and giving it a reassuring tap. "You're going to miss the train." Giles nodded towards the platform where the signalman had just given his final 'all aboard'.

"Goodness! Well, goodbye then." She turned and ran as swiftly as dignity allowed towards the train where her employer, Lord Midnight Gunn, stood waiting, holding their carriage door open.

"Miss Carmichael." Midnight acknowledged her with a wry look as she hurried past him and sprang into the compartment. Midnight hopped in after her and just managed to close the door when the train lurched forward and the Special Scotch Express began its slow acceleration away from London King's Cross Station. Steam billowed past their carriage window, temporarily blotting out the forms of Mr. Morgan and a very melancholy Mrs. Clementine Phillips who was dabbing her eyes with a handkerchief.

"Sorry," Agnes said to Midnight as she sat down, straightened her skirts, then adjusted her hat. Midnight sat opposite her, next to his adopted daughter, Polly.

"Not to worry. You made it in time. Just," he added with the smallest hint of disapproval. Punctuality was something he took great pride in, but he often had to remind himself that not everyone held it in the same regard as he did, and so he tried not to sound too critical.

Polly jumped up from her seat and pulled down the sash window. She held onto her bonnet with the stump of her left arm, her hand having being amputated some years ago, and stuck her head out to shout through the clouds of steam.

"See ya, Missus P. Mista' Morgan! Don't be too sad wivout us, eh?" She gave a last vigorous wave with her right hand and plonked herself back in her seat with a loud huff.

Midnight closed the window then fished out a crumpled newspaper from the rack on the carriage wall. Eyeing Polly, he said, "I see the elocution lessons are progressing well."

"It takes more than a few months to break the habit of a lifetime," Agnes replied, a little defensive. "Polly is doing very well with her instructions. She's a very bright young miss. Quite intuitive, in fact."

"That, Miss Carmichael, is somewhat of an understatement," Midnight said, flashing a look of amusement at Polly's governess.

"It's excitin', init, Aggie? I ain't never been on a train before." Polly beamed at Agnes then at her father who was regarding her with one eyebrow cocked. She stopped grinning and cleared her throat. "I mean. It is exciting, is it not, Miss Agg... I mean, Miss Carmichael. Happen I have never been on a train before." She stole a sideways glance at Midnight who was smiling broadly into his newspaper.

"It is exciting, darling. Although, I think you may change your mind by the time we get to Edinburgh."

"Why? Is Edinbo- Edinburo- Edin..." She gave up trying to pronounce it as eloquently as her governess had. "Is it 'orrible there?"

Miss Carmichael's mouth twitched at the corner. It didn't help matters when, out of the corner of her eye, she could see that the newspaper strategically placed to hide her employer's face was shaking. Lord Gunn was clearly struggling to hold in his laughter.

"Well, I was referring to the length of the journey. I have never been to Scotland, Polly. But I'm sure it's not horrible. Is it, sir?"

Her direct address forced Midnight to lower his paper, revealing his mirthful expression. "Indeed, it is not. Edinburgh is very beautiful, for the most part. The castle is especially spectacular. There are, however, some areas that might qualify as significantly squalid, but that is the case in most cities, I'm afraid. And it is worth noting that even those places are beautiful in their own way."

Polly wrinkled her nose. "What, like the docks, ya mean? 'Cause them docks is proper filthy and stinky. I 'member some right old bleedin'—"

"Quite enough, thank you, young lady." Midnight shook out his newspaper and fixed Polly with a remonstrative glare. Polly, he was pleased to see, looked suitably abashed.

"Sorry, Papa. I forget meself sometimes, forget I'm supposed to be a lady now and not a muckspout." She gazed at him from under her long, sweeping lashes, and he melted.

He found it very hard to chastise her, and if it were just him and Polly at home, he wouldn't mind her cockney twang so much. It was part of who she was, and he loved her all the more for her character. But he had a responsibility to raise her as a young lady of means should be raised. One day she would be a debutant and a fully-fledged member of society—perish the thought—and she couldn't be running around cursing like a street urchin then.

It had been seventeen months since the Christmas of 1860 when Midnight had adopted Polly. Since she had no birth certificate, they'd decided together that her official birthday would be Christmas Eve. Polly had voiced that she'd 'very much like to be eight' that particular year because that's how old she thought she might be, even though 'Evan, one of the bleeders from the docks, was always tellin' me I was a forty-foot!' Midnight knew the expression 'forty-foot' to be a derisive taunt for a short person, and he could see how much it had meant to Polly to be an eight-year-old. He'd thought it about right anyway, judging from what Mrs. P. had told him of her sister's grand-children. Of course, this Christmas would see her into double figures, and Polly thought that was really something to celebrate.

Midnight roused himself from his reminiscent state and focused on reading his newspaper. Polly fell silent and took to gazing out of the window, twiddling her thumbs and swinging her legs back and forth. Miss Carmichael took out a book from her bag and settled in for the ten-and-a-half-hour journey ahead. The Special Scotch Express departed daily from King's Cross at 10 o'clock sharp and was expected to arrive at Edinburgh, Waverley station at half-past eight in the evening its counterpart departed from Waverley simultaneously, and the two trains were expected to pass each other roughly halfway through the journey. There would be a brief twenty-minute stopover at York for light refreshments and toilet facilities. But knowing how poor the infamous 'railway sandwiches' were, Midnight had asked Mrs. P, his cook and housekeeper, to prepare two lunch baskets for the journey: one basket for himself, Polly and Agnes, and another for Laura Carter, his housemaid, and Charlie Fenwick, his stable hand-come temporary valet. Giles, his old butler and friend, wasn't travelling with him this time. He and Mrs. P. were staying in London as neither of them felt quite up to the long journey and Giles had been entrusted with the supervision of the charitable hospital renovation in his master's absence. It was an unusual relationship between master and employee; Giles had been Josiah Gunn's confidant, too, and had carried on that role after Lord Gunn senior's untimely death. Midnight trusted Giles beyond all others. Miss Carter and Charlie were in the next carriage along. Midnight had thought it prudent to book two carriages, fearing that five people together in a small space for ten hours might be a little cramped.

It had only taken a little over an hour for Polly to become bored.

"Is it lunchtime yet?" she asked of no one in particular.

Midnight took out his pocket watch and checked the time. "It's barely past eleven, little miss. Are you hungry already?"

"Starvin'! Mrs. P. had me get up right early this mornin' for breakfast." She looked longingly at the lunch basket on the overhead racking.

"If we eat lunch now, there will be nothing to see us

through the rest of the journey. I won't be buying refreshments at York."

"I believe Mrs. Phillips packed some scones and jam as well as a substantial lunch," Agnes said. "I admit to being rather peckish myself."

"A valid point. There's bound to be food in abundance if Mrs. P. packed it. Very well. Let's have a look and see what delights await us, shall we?" Midnight rose and took down the wicker basket, which was surprisingly heavy. "By the weight of this thing, I think she must have packed several pound cakes." He grunted. Placing the basket on the seat between himself and Polly, he opened it. It was crammed full to bursting with cake, scones, bottles of elderflower cordial, cold meats, eggs, bread, and cheese, and—he was very pleased to discover—a whole pork pie and a jar of plum chutney.

"Mmm!" Polly moaned, her eyes widening with glee.

"Just the scones and jam for now. We shall save the rest just in case the hotel doesn't serve food that late."

There were four small tea plates and four sets of cutlery strapped to the inside of the basket's lid. Midnight extracted three plates and three knives. He handed one set to Agnes and one to Polly, who was jiggling up and down on the seat, eagerly awaiting her mid-morning treat. He unwrapped the scones and offered them around, then opened the jar of jam. Midnight sliced Polly's scone in half and went to spread the jam on for her, but she stopped him.

"I'll do it meself," she said stubbornly, wielding her knife. Midnight placed the jar on the seat next to her. He knew how independent she was; she had taken care of herself for years on the streets of London and she hated being mollycoddled. Polly dipped her knife into the red, sticky mixture and scooped out a large dollop. The train rocked, causing the precariously balanced glob to fall off the knife and land on her lap. Agnes put down her own plate and moved to assist the girl, but Midnight put up his hand to stop her. Polly's lips were set in a thin, determined line. She scraped the jam from her dress, smearing it deep into the fabric, and dumped it unceremoniously atop one half of her scone. Her second attempt was more successful. The train behaved itself, and she managed to garnish the second slice without incident. With a satisfied expression, she dropped her knife into the basket, grabbed the scone and took a giant bite. Her mouth was rammed full of the tasty treat, but she still managed a crumbly grin for her father.

He reciprocated with a broad grin of his own and passed the jam to Agnes who was eyeing the strawberry smear on Polly's dress with concern. "It will wash out. Don't worry," he whispered. And if it didn't, he would buy her a new dress. He would buy as many dresses as it took for his daughter to feel confident and capable.

After the basket had been re-packed and put away and a full bottle of cordial had been shared out, Agnes buried her head back in her book and Midnight picked up the newspaper once again. Polly was playing happily with her cup and ball toy, and the rhythmic sound of the train wheels on the tracks was permeated by the sharp knock of wood on wood every time Polly swung the dangling ball and tried to catch it in the cup. The train swayed from side to side, and Midnight grew tired of the paper. He folded it and put it back in the rack.

"Can I read it, Papa?"

"I shouldn't think there would be much in it to interest you, little one," Midnight said but reached for it nonetheless. "Here. You can practice your letters and read aloud to me."

Polly took the paper, unfolded it, and spread it out on the seat. She knelt on the floor of the carriage so as to allow for the fact that she couldn't hold the broadsheet out in front of her like her father had. She crossed her arms and rested them on the edge of the seat scanning the columns for something interesting to practice with. Midnight leaned his head back on the seat, eyes closed, as Polly began to narrate in stuttering snippets.

"As the nor... northern b-l-o-c-k-a-d-e. Blockade?"

"Mm-hm."

"As the northern blockade of southern ports con... con-tin-you-ez?"

"Continues," Midnight corrected, not needing to look.

"—continues, it is said that the pro-duc-tion—production of ships for the Am-er-i-can war effort falls to Li-ver-pool where sour-says?"

"Sources."

"—sources say that secret plans are afoot to launch a series of naval cru... c-r-u-i-s-e-r-s. What's that say?"

"Cruisers," Agnes piped in. She'd put her book down and was listening intently to what Polly was reading.

"A sloop named The CSS Alabama is ex-pec-ted to launch in July this year," Polly finished and huffed out a big breath.

Midnight reached out to pull one of her curls. "Excellent, dear one. Your reading is very much improved."

"May I have that, darling?" Agnes asked Polly, pointing at the newspaper. Polly nodded and carefully folded it in half then handed it to her. "Thank you." Agnes quickly found the article Polly had been reading.

Midnight noted her anxiety as her eyes passed quickly over the report. "You must be worried, Miss Carmichael. Have you heard from home recently?"

"Nothing from Daddy since the end of March. I gave Mr. Morgan a letter for New York this morning, begging Daddy to send word of my brothers. I haven't had a letter from Andrew or Billy since January."

"Perhaps the blockade is preventing any letters from reaching your father. It will be difficult for mail to find its way to England too. I suppose it also depends on which state your brothers are deployed to at the moment. They may not be able to get mail out."

"Yes. Daddy said as much in his last letter. It's just that five months is a long time to be waiting to see if they are still alive." Her voice broke a little, and she cleared her throat.

Midnight reached forward and patted her hand. "Bad news travels faster, Miss Carmichael. Take some comfort in that. I'm sure that once your father receives your letter, he will do his best to address your concerns."

"I hope so. I wish this blasted war was over."

"But then you'd leave us," Polly chimed in, her little brow creased.

"I don't want to leave you, child. It's lovely being back in England. I just..." She couldn't finish her sentence.

"Miss your home and family?" Midnight offered.

"Yes." Agnes fished out a handkerchief and dabbed away the tears that had begun to form.

Polly jumped up and flung her arms around Agnes, squeezing her tight. "We're your 'ome and family then, least until you get back to yours. Don't cry, Aggie."

"Bless you, darling. Thank you. That means a lot."

"She is right, of course. You are entrusted to my care as long as your father requires it of me. We shall do our best to make your stay with us as homely as possible."

In the summer of 1861, Midnight had received an overseas letter from a Mr. Richard Carmichael, introducing himself as an old friend and business associate of the late Josiah Gunn. Giles Morgan had confirmed this when Midnight had asked, declaring him to be 'one of the more decent fellows that your father knew'. In his letter, Carmichael had explained that his two sons had joined the union army to fight the confederate south and that as battles raged in the state of New York and the rest of the country, he feared for his daughter's safety. His daughter, Agnes, was an educated but unmarried woman of twenty-three, and with his sons gone, he feared what would happen to her if he should die, for his health was not as it once was. He wrote to enquire if Mr. Gunn knew of anyone in London who might be willing to take his daughter on as a governess or companion to a lady for the duration of the war. Midnight immediately wrote back that he was himself looking to appoint a governess for his newly adopted daughter and that he would gladly pay passage for Agnes Carmichael to attend them as soon as possible. Since Polly's adoption, Midnight had hired several governesses, none of whom seemed the right fit. They had all been much older and very 'strict and crabby', as Polly had put it. He'd taken a chance on Agnes, hoping that a younger woman might connect better with his daughter. And he'd been right. Agnes had just the right mix of empathy and discipline to maintain control over Polly's impetuous, rambunctious personality without seeming to smother it. The situation worked well. He had concerns, though—namely what would happen to Polly when the war ended and Agnes went back to America. Of course, Agnes would be pleased to go home and Midnight could then relax a little. His household had doubled since Polly's arrival and now he had the added pressure of ensuring that he maintained control over his powers at all times, both at home and in public. The people who knew of his special abilities were few and Agnes was not one of them. He no longer had the liberty of the odd slip up as he had done when it was just himself, his butler, and his cook. Midnight had kept himself in the shadows his entire life, and learning to adapt to a certain lack of privacy and the continued suppression of his powers was proving more frustrating than he'd anticipated.

1

ARRIVAL

The train had been thirty minutes late pulling into Waverley. Midnight now stood on the platform, surrounded by their luggage, and clicked his tongue impatiently. He compared his pocket watch against the time displayed on the station clock.

"Nine o'clock. I do hope Ms. Adams's driver has waited for us."

"Charlie's coming back, look!" Polly said and pointed towards the exit where Charlie Fenwick was hurrying towards them.

He reached them and, panting a little, declared that their carriage waited outside.

"Thank goodness," Miss Carter said. "I shouldn't have liked to try to find rooms in the city this late."

"You could've bunked in wiv me, Laura. I wouldn't 'ave minded," Polly piped up.

The housemaid smiled at her. "I know, Miss Polly, but I shouldn't think Miss Carmichael would want to be sharing her bed with the both of us, now would she, eh?"

"You wouldn't mind, would ya, Aggie?" Polly turned swiftly to her governess who shook her head.

"Had the carriage not been here, I really wouldn't have minded at all."

"However," Midnight interrupted, "it is here, and we really shouldn't delay any longer. I'm sure Miss Carter and Charlie are tired and anxious to be on their way. Miss Carmichael, would you stay by the exit with Polly while I help Charlie to the carriage with the luggage?"

"Of course, sir."

"Ready when you are, my man." Midnight indicated to the porter who immediately began wheeling their trolley full of belongings to the exit where all the private carriages and cabs were patiently waiting for passengers. The five of them followed. It was raining outside, so Polly and Agnes stayed by the exit under the protection of the awning while Midnight helped Miss Carter into the private carriage that had been sent by his distant cousin, Ms. Felicity Adams.

"Thank you, sir. You're very kind." Miss Carter smiled sweetly.

"Not at all." Midnight replied. He caught her gaze and held it a second too long. Catching himself, he quickly looked away and went to supervise the loading of the heavy trunks on the rear of the carriage. Their luggage now safely secured, Charlie hopped on the front seat with the driver, shucking the collar of his long coat up around his ears and fixing his flat cap to his head in a vain attempt to ward off the rain. Midnight tipped the porter and went to have a word with the driver. The two horses whinnied and shifted uneasily as he approached.

"Whoa, there! Starlight, Gorgon, whoa!" The driver steadied the team and turned to Midnight. "I'm sorry, sir. I dinnae know what's got the buggers spooked so. Must be the storm, aye?"

"Indeed," Midnight replied and backed away a step. "Please inform Ms. Adams that I and the rest of my party will be arriving tomorrow evening. If she could send the carriage to The Royal Hotel, number fifty-three Princes Street for three o'clock? I should be done with my business then. My valet and housemaid will travel with you tonight and ready the cottage."

"Aye, sir," the driver said, doffing his cap.

"Goodbye, sir. No need to worry. We'll 'ave everyfin' ready for ya," said Charlie.

"Safe travels, Charlie. See you both tomorrow."

The driver clicked the reins and the carriage moved slowly away. Midnight stood on the pavement, the rain trickling down the neck of his coat, and watched it go. Just as the carriage began to turn a corner, he caught a brief glimpse of Miss Carter at the window. She appeared to be crying. His brow wrinkled, as he wondered what on earth had caused her to be upset. Nothing had been said that could've prompted her tears, of that he was sure. Perhaps she was just overwhelmed at being so far from home. She had said that she'd never been outside of London before. Yes, that must be it.

Midnight checked his pocket watch; the time was now twenty-five past nine. He looked back at Polly and Agnes. Polly was leaning against her governess and yawning. It was past her usual bedtime and she was tired. The porter had told him that The Royal Hotel was only a short distance across from the station and down the street. There wasn't much point in taking a cab, despite the rain. They only had two small overnight bags between them now. He could carry

Polly and one of the bags. Miss Carmichael could carry the other.

They set off down the darkened street, the dim light of the gas lamps did nothing to aid their way through the heavy rain. Their coats did little to protect them from the weather either. Early May in Scotland was not the same as early May in London; there was a distinct chill in the air. It wasn't long before he could see the lights of the hotel some four hundred yards away on the opposite side of Princes Street. There was a narrow alley to his right. As they passed by it, he thought he heard a low snarl. Instinct told him to look.

He peered into the gloom. There were no gas lamps in the alley. Fat droplets of rain bounced off the ground and off the jumble of indeterminable articles that littered the narrow space, making it very difficult to see anything clearly. His skin prickled in warning. His unique senses told him that deep in the shadows, something was staring back.

It wasn't safe here. That much he knew. He was not afraid for himself. If he'd been alone, he would've thought nothing of venturing into the dark to confront whatever awaited. But he had his daughter and Miss Carmichael to consider, the latter having no notion of his distinctive set of skills.

A noise came suddenly out of the dark, and he thought he saw something or someone fall to the ground. Another shape, large and hunched, pounced on top of it. Midnight heard a muffled shout.

"Ho! Who's there?" he shouted back, the rain distorting his voice. "Ho!" There was no reply. All of his senses were on heightened alert now. The touch of a hand on his sleeve startled him.

"What is it?" Agnes whispered.

"I think someone is in trouble." He glanced quickly around. They were alone and The Royal was still some way down the road. He couldn't risk it. Even in this weather, Agnes might see him move the shadows. Not only that, but he had no idea what adversary he might face. He couldn't put her or Polly directly in the path of danger unnecessarily. "Let's get to the hotel and I'll send word to the police."

Agnes needed no encouragement. She set off at a quick pace, anxious to put some distance between herself and whatever trouble was in the alley. Midnight followed, clutching his sleepy daughter to him protectively. As he reached the corner of Princes Street, he glanced back just in time to see a pair of glowing eyes set high in the shadow of something huge and distinctly beast-like retreat back into the refuge of the dark alley.

His own secret power called to him, primal instinct urging him to answer, but he repressed the desire. He was in control of the shadows and the light, and now was not the time to put on a show. He stared at the spot where the shadowy shape had been, long enough to ensure nothing was following them, then hurriedly escorted his two charges to the welcoming lights and safety of The Royal Hotel.

Midnight heard Agnes sigh when they entered the hotel's foyer. Her sense of relief echoed his own. He put Polly, who looked about ready to drop with exhaustion, down on the chaise nearest the reception desk and went to register with the clerk. Once he had the two room keys, one for himself and the other for Agnes and Polly, he asked the clerk where the nearest police station was.

"We've a runner, sir, if you need to send word?"

"Yes. I do. I need to report an attack."

"Aye, sir. If you can write your message on this paper, I'll have our lad take it down the road." The clerk immediately

handed him the necessaries to pen his summons. "Are you
and your party all right, sir? Can I have some tea brought to
you?"

"Yes, thank you. We're unhurt. It was not us that suffered
the attack. I'm a witness. So if you could inform me when a
constable arrives?" He handed the note to the clerk, who
then rang a brass bell above the counter. "Tea would be
most welcome for myself and Miss Carmichael, and a hot
cocoa for my daughter, if you could?"

"Of course, sir. I'll have it sent up shortly."

A young lad of about fifteen appeared, and the clerk
handed him Midnight's note along with instructions to
deliver it to the Edinburgh City Police. The lad stuffed the
note into his inside coat pocket and sped off into the night.
Midnight had a twinge of worry, hoping the youngster
didn't fall foul of whatever he had seen in the alley. Perhaps
he should have gone himself. He looked back at Polly, who
was now gently snoring on the chaise, her damp clothes
clinging to her, and her dark curls plastered to her
cherubic cheeks. He sighed. He would have to carry her
upstairs and settle her into bed. Miss Carmichael would
need help.

"Come along, Polly Peeps," he said gently as he scooped
her up. "Miss Carmichael, would you be so kind as to get the
door? I'll help you get her settled before the police arrive."

The Royal's rooms were very pleasant—spacious but
cosy. Miss Carmichael's was a twin room. Midnight laid the
sleeping child on the closest of the two beds while Agnes
began unpacking Polly's night clothes from her bag. He took
off Polly's shoes and put them on the floor, then stripped off
her soggy coat and hung it over a chair back to dry. There
was a linen towel by the wash stand, which he took to dry
off her damp hair; the last thing he wanted was for her to

catch a cold. Polly roused a little while he rubbed her hair and patted her face dry.

"Is it mornin' already?" she asked, her small voice heavy with sleep.

"No, child. It's bed time, but you need to sit up and put on your night gown before you catch a chill."

She did as she was told, and he and Agnes managed to rid her of her wet clothes and tuck her up under the soft eiderdown just as somebody knocked on the door.

"Room service," came a muffled voice from the corridor. Midnight let the maid in with the tea tray.

"Oh. Apologies, sir. Martha has taken your tea to your own room. Should I have her bring it here, then?" she said sheepishly looking at Agnes then back to Midnight.

"No need." Midnight coughed. "I was just helping Miss Carmichael get my daughter ready for bed. I shall retire to my own room presently."

"Aye, sir," the maid said and bobbed a curtsey. She put the tea tray down on the coffee table. "Will there be anything else?"

"No, thank you," he said. She bobbed again and left.

Avoiding Agnes's eyes, Midnight took the steaming mug of cocoa and handed it to Polly. "Drink this, sweetheart. It will warm you up nicely. Are you hungry? We still have a little cake left."

Polly took a glug of the hot, milky drink and sighed in satisfaction. She licked her lips, but a moustache of froth still remained, making Midnight smile.

"I ain't hungry, thank you. I'm just flagged out. I di'n't know Scotland was this far from 'ome."

"Finish your cocoa, and then you can sleep." He tugged one of her curls. "Good night, Miss Peeps."

"Night, Papa."

Midnight stood to address Agnes. "The police should be here soon, and I shall have to go to the alley. Hopefully I won't be too long. If you need anything in the meantime, ask the clerk at the front desk. Sleep well, Miss Carmichael."

"Good night, sir. And... be careful."

Midnight smiled, appreciating her concern.

He was barely in his own room five minutes when the message came that two members of the local constabulary were waiting for him downstairs. He took one quick gulp of his tea, put his damp coat back on, and headed down to greet them.

"Good evening, constables. Lord Gunn," he said, introducing himself and holding out his hand. He rarely used his official title but found that being a Lord sometimes had its advantages. It certainly made the two policemen pay attention.

"Evenin', your lordship. Constable MacKay." He shook Midnight's hand. "And this is Constable Rogers." His colleague nodded and reached for Midnight's hand. "We got word of an attack near the train station? What can you tell us?"

"Yes. I saw something on my way to the hotel. I heard somebody shouting. It looked like there was trouble."

"I see," MacKay said. He'd taken out his notepad and pencil and was busily jotting down details. "What time was this?"

"Around nine-thirty, I believe."

"Can you tell us which street, sir?" Rogers asked.

"I'm afraid I didn't see a street name. I can show you though."

"Aye, all right. Best to be cautious though, sir. You need to stay behind us, just in case."

"Of course, Constable," Midnight replied with practiced consternation.

They set off into the rain, Midnight ensuring he kept behind the two policemen as instructed, not because he needed their protection, but rather because they might need his. Better to stay behind and perform any necessary actions from the rear where the constables were less likely to see what he was doing. They arrived at the spot a few minutes later.

"Down there." Midnight pointed to the alley.

"Stay here with Rogers, please, your lordship. I'll go take a look." MacKay was on alert as he stepped slowly towards the ominous entrance. He stopped just short of a foot away and shouted. "Hello? Is anyone down there?" When no reply came, he proceeded into the darkness and disappeared.

Midnight and Rogers peered into the gloom after him until they could make out MacKay's shadowy form stumbling clumsily over the slippery cobbles and piles of rubbish that were strewn across the alley. MacKay kicked something metallic with his boot; the subsequent clanging rang out like a church bell in the night.

"Are ye alright, Mac?" Rogers called, taking a tentative step forward.

"Aye. Just cannae tell ma arse from ma elbow, it's so bloody dark."

The rain continued to pelt down. Midnight thought that soon it would be pointless wearing any clothes at all save for his modesty, for they offered little protection from the deluge.

MacKay called to him. "How far down, your lordship?"

"Not too far; about where you are, I should say." He concentrated, feeling for the shadows that courted him incessantly in case he should need to call on them, but his senses told him there was no imminent danger, not like before. Whatever had been here was gone, he was sure of that.

"Och, bollocks!" MacKay cursed. "Found him! Dead as a bloody doornail too, aye."

Rogers and Midnight advanced towards MacKay. As they neared, and their eyes adjusted to the murkiness, two shapes emerged. MacKay was standing, hands on his hips, over an indistinct tangle of cloth and limbs. He lifted up his booted foot and pushed at the hefty lump, causing it to roll over.

"Holy Christ!" Rogers declared and gagged. The saccharine scent of iron and other bodily fluids lay heavy in the damp night air. MacKay put a hand out to halt Midnight's advance.

"Stay back, sir. I need to secure the scene. Besides, it's not something a gentleman should witness."

"It's all right, Constable. I've seen worse, I can assure you." This statement earned him a questioning look from MacKay. 'I've a friend at Scotland Yard. I know the procedure," was all he said. He thought it best not to elaborate.

"Oh. I see," MacKay replied, frowning. Then, turning to Rogers he said, "Go fetch the Inspector before you lose your guts, and tell the cart to come, too." Rogers scurried off, his hand covering his mouth. "Bloody greenie, that one," MacKay said nodding his head in the direction in which his colleague had just fled. "Unlike you, though, eh? I can see this isn't your first dead body. Ah, dinnae know that I've heard of a lord being friends with anyone from the police force before. Unless you mean the commissioner, of course?" Mackay eyed him a little suspiciously.

"No, not him. I'm somewhat of an amateur sleuth, you

might say. I take an interest, that's all." Midnight shrugged, hoping to discourage further questioning from the constable. He was dying to get his hands on the body and see what he could glean from this man's last moments. From the looks of it, something had ripped out the man's throat, and there were huge gashes in his face and on his hands where, presumably, he'd tried to defend himself. He needed a distraction and fast. Once Rogers brought reinforcements, he'd never get a chance to touch the body and his curiosity was peaked.

"What do you think made those marks?" Midnight asked, causing the constable to cease his scrutiny and refocus on the dead man.

"Looks like another animal attack to me. Throat's been ripped to shreds, aye?" said MacKay.

"Another? Have there been more like this?"

"Oh, aye. Only the one, mind. Found a body in a similar condition just last week. Down by the docks, it was. Not my division, you ken. But word travels, and we've been told to keep a look out for a rabid dog. Inspector Anderson thinks it's a stowaway from one of the boats. Have a mind if you're wandering around the city late at night, aye?"

"Hmm. A rabid dog, you say?" Must be one hell of a big dog, he thought. He *must* get his hands on this dead man.

The constable began cautiously poking around the surrounding area, looking for any evidence. This was Midnight's chance. He summoned the waiting shadows, controlling the insistent surge within him and letting them in slowly. He didn't want MacKay to notice the way the shadows began to swirl and thicken as they inched their way towards him and seeped through his flesh. It was still painful when the dark power roiled inside of him, but he could bear it now that he'd learned to balance it with light.

Midnight concentrated on a spot some distance away down the alley and projected a thin tendril of smoke from his palm to creep along the cobbles. Once past the constable, Midnight pushed the smoke hard until it collided with a wooden palette, causing it to come crashing down. MacKay jumped, and Midnight continued the play.

"There! look! I think I saw someone. It might be a witness or the killer."

"Stay here, and don't move," MacKay said and set off down the alley in pursuit shouting, "Halt! City police. Halt in the name of the law!"

Midnight quickly crouched low over the body and laid his hand on the bloodied, disfigured face. He closed his eyes and entered the mind of the victim, ready to witness the man's last moments from his point of view.

There was nothing.

He forced another tendril of the shadows into the man's brain but, again, found nothing.

How very odd. It was the first time he had never been able to discern memories from a body and he did not like it. This man had clearly been murdered and brutally; his throat lay in tattered ribbons of tissue and sinew. Midnight distinctly remembered somebody shouting when he had seen the beastly shape lunge at the prostate form on the ground not forty minutes earlier. This victim's memories should be fresh and easily accessible. So, why couldn't he see? Had his powers weakened from being suppressed these last months since Miss Carmichael had come to stay? He stood up, puzzled and more than a little disconcerted.

MacKay returned, panting slightly. "Canny see anything. The alley comes out near the bridge, so I bet the bastard's fled. Are ye all right, your lordship? Did ye see anything?"

"No, constable. Not a damned thing."

2

RUMORS AND REMONSTRATIONS

F elicity Adams's driver was outside The Royal Hotel at precisely five minutes before three the next afternoon. Midnight was thankful to see that it was not raining. In fact, the sun had put in an appearance quite early this morning and had decided to stay for the duration. This was good news, because his long coat was still too damp to wear as a result of the previous evening's events. He had been forced to travel to the lawyer's office this morning in just his suit and jacket, minus his top hat, which just looked odd without the long overcoat.

Polly *had* caught a chill and had begun sneezing quite violently after breakfast, causing Agnes to become extremely flustered and insist on a trip to the pharmacist at once for something to reduce the fever. While she was gone, Midnight had sat the little girl on his knee, wrapped her in a blanket and sent healing light into her shivering body. Within minutes, she was feeling much better, which strangely hadn't done much to appease the very-much-put-out Miss Carmichael upon her return.

'Must've got some dust up me nose, Aggie,' Polly had

said, shrugging, at which point, Agnes herself had begun to sneeze and feel quite unwell. 'Least you got some medicine, eh?' Polly had said trying to be helpful but only earning herself a look of remonstration from her governess.

Midnight discovered, to his detriment, that Agnes was not the most pleasant company when she wasn't feeling well and had a rambunctious, miraculously-cured nine-year-old to look after. He'd been relieved to be on his way by eleven-thirty for his luncheon with the lawyer. The consultation had gone very well, despite him having to liaise with the firm's legal secretary instead of Mr. Rosemont, whom, he had been informed, was 'indisposed indefinitely' at present. Either way, he had left the morning meeting with a brief-case full of prospective properties to mull over during the journey to the cottage.

Constable MacKay had taken the address of Samach House, the cottage on the Glenhaven Estate where Midnight would be spending the majority of the summer. 'Just in case we need to be in touch,' he'd said. He'd dismissed Lord Gunn with a handshake and a 'Thank you for being a good citizen' once Rogers had returned accompanied by Inspector Anderson. For once, Midnight was pleased to not have to get involved with the investigation. Anderson had confirmed the police suspicions of there being a rabid dog on the loose. 'Some kind of wolfhound,' he reckoned.

And so, despite his misgivings regarding the victims' absent memories, Midnight had left them to it, ready to enjoy his summer of house-hunting and frivolity with Polly and to leave the policing to someone else.

"*Achoo!*" sneezed Agnes for about the twentieth time since they'd set off for Glenhaven.

"Bless you," said Polly, matching her blessings with every sneeze.

"Oh. What rotten luck that I should catch a cold right at the start of our holiday," Agnes bemoaned.

"Indeed. Not to worry, Miss Carmichael. We shall be there soon enough, and I'll have Miss Carter make you something to take away the chill."

"I am so very cold. I shall be glad of a hot drink." Agnes sniffed and blew her nose on a well-used handkerchief.

Midnight felt a little guilty about her suffering; he could've healed her within the blink of an eye, but she knew nothing of his powers and he could not risk anymore people knowing his secrets.

He mentally ticked off the list of people who knew what he was capable of: Giles and Mrs. P.—they'd always known and been the only ones for a long time who had. Then, some seven years ago now, Inspector Gredge had made his acquaintance, quite by accident, during the case of the Peckham Vampire—something they'd both been investigating and had inadvertently ended up in a life-threatening situation. Midnight had used his dark power to save Gredge's life, and it hadn't seemed wise to attempt to erase the Inspector's memory. Midnight had been younger then and not in full control of his powers—anything could've gone wrong. He had a brief flashback to Chinese Mary, the madam whose mind he'd scrambled and who had subsequently died at the hands of his enemy. Mary was proof that memory wiping wasn't something with which he should ever be meddling. He shivered at the thought of that poor woman's fate and went back to his list. After Gredge, it'd been Constable Rowe whose loyalty to his superior, Gredge, had proved useful. Polly came next, who, it turned out, had unique powers of her own. Then it had been Miss Carter and Charlie Fenwick, whose souls he had rescued. And lastly, Hemlock Nightingale, the man from whom he rescued said souls after helping Gredge solve the murder of a wealthy aristocrat.

That was one detestable creature whose head he wished he could've meddled with. He'd heard nothing of Hemlock in the eighteen months since finding the villain's battered demon-goggles on his front doorstep. It was something that continued to cause him the odd sleepless night. A body had never been found during the search of the Thames, and Midnight lived with the ominous feeling that perhaps his enemy hadn't perished in the freezing river that night. Hemlock was the one person whom Midnight wished knew nothing of his own, dark secrets... or Polly's. One of the reasons he'd brought them all to Scotland for the summer was to get far away from London and the lingering night-mares Nightingale's actions had bestowed on them. He could protect Polly much better out here, away from the hustle and bustle of the grimy streets of the capital. The fresh air and sunshine would do them all good too.

Although, from his view out of the carriage window, he saw the sky beginning to cloud over again. Midnight banged on the roof of the carriage, pulled down the window hatch and stuck out his head to speak to the driver.

"How much further to Glenhaven?"

"About another hour I'd say, sir. We'll be there afore dusk," the driver replied over his shoulder.

"Papa? I need to go."

Midnight glanced back at the little girl who was fidgeting in her seat, legs crossed. "You can't wait until we reach the cottage?"

"Nah. I can't hold it no more. The bumps in the road are making it worse."

Midnight sighed and shouted to the driver to stop. The carriage lurched to a halt, and Midnight opened the door, descended down the steps, and held out his hand to Polly. He was about to ask Agnes to go with her but the governess was now shivering under a blanket. He couldn't very well go himself; the girl needed her privacy. There was nothing for it, she'd just have to go on her own.

"Sweetheart, will you be all right on your own? Poor Miss Carmichael isn't exactly in a fit state to be outside in this breeze." Indeed, a hearty breeze had set in along with the ever-dimming sky. "Just pop behind that tree by the road, and don't wander any further. Can you manage that?"

"'Course I can," she said, hopping from one foot to the other and grimacing.

Midnight could see that her need was indeed urgent. "Off you pop, then. Shout if you need me."

She ran off towards the big Scots pine about five meters from the edge of the road. Midnight shut the door to the carriage to keep Agnes from the wind. He drifted over to chat with the driver who sat patiently, cooing to his horses. They whinnied upon Midnight's approach.

"I never asked your name, good man."

"Bobby MacDonald, sir. Most folks just call me Bobby Mac."

"These are fine horses, Bobby Mac. What breed are they?" he asked, looking over the two-strong team appraisingly. He wasn't overly fond of horses himself. He could ride—his father had taught him—but he held no particular affection for the animals; horses never quite seemed comfortable in his presence. Asking Bobby Mac about the horses was just a way of making conversation. He was eager to find out more about his mysterious distant relative, Felicity Adams. Usually the best people to ask were the staff. One could tell a lot about a person's character by how they treated their employees. Even if Bobby Mac sang her praises, Midnight would be able to sense if he was lying.

"They're both Flemish and Cleveland crosses. Starlight —she's the mare—she's two years older than Gorgon. She keeps him in line usually. He can be a bit headstrong, especially when he's being rigged up. But they're both good, strong carriage horses."

"Does Ms. Adams keep many horses?"

"Not as many as she used to, aye. We had a four-strong team last year as well as the racing stock. But since the master's death, the mistress saw fit to sell on his favourites on account of she found the memories too painful to bear. We have these two—" He indicated to the carriage horses. "—a fine Spanish Jennet—that's the mistress's horse—and an Arabian Kochlaini. Samson's his name. He's a bloody beast of a horse. Does nae like being ridden much; he'll gi' ye a nasty bite if he gets the chance. Do you ride, sir?"

"Only if I have to. It's not one of my favourite pursuits, I have to admit. My father held an interest in horses though. A Kochlaini, you say? Aren't those incredibly rare in Britain?"

"Aye, sir. Samson's only been with us two years. The master won him in a poker game just a year before he died. He was a good rider, an enthusiast. No doubt he would've broken him had he had more time. The mistress has ridden him a few times, but the stallion's not over keen, aye."

"Why doesn't she sell him on, like the others?"

"Och she's not sentimental over Samson. She's determined to crack the bugger is all. Does nae like to be defeated."

"A determined young woman then, your mistress?"

"You could say that, aye." Bobby Mac gave a wry smile,

and Midnight could sense no falsehood or unease coming from him.

A sudden crack of thunder barreled through the sky, making them both jump. Midnight looked up and saw that the clouding skies and sunshine had turned ominously dark. He felt the first spatter of rain on his cheeks and remembered Polly. He jerked himself around to face the tree behind which she had disappeared to relieve herself. She wasn't making her way back yet. Surely, she should be done by now.

"Polly?" he shouted over the stiff breeze that was now tugging at his coat tails. "Hurry, child. You're going to get soaked through!" *Again,* he thought. The girl had left her coat in the carriage, and he couldn't warm her in the presence of Bobby Mac and Agnes. "Polly!" His shout was a little more insistent this time. *Dammit! Where was she?*

"Is everything all right, sir?" Agnes poked her head out of the sash window, eyes, bleary, her nose red and swollen.

"Everything's fine," he snapped, not meaning to sound so abrupt but for that twist of fear in his gut that every parent feels when their child is suddenly out of sight and unresponsive. "I'll go fetch her. Stay out of the rain, Miss Carmichael."

Agnes dutifully shut the window and sank gratefully back into her blanket while Midnight tramped impatiently through the long grass towards the large Scots pine. When he reached the tree and found there was no sign of his daughter, the twist of fear became a full-blown stab of panic. Lightening flashed overhead as thunder rolled across the blackening sky once again and the rain fell in heavy drops. Midnight stood a few feet from the pine looking frantically around for any sign of Polly. How far could a nine-year-old get in the space of two minutes?

He spotted a dip in the field about twenty meters away and could see the leafy tops of a small copse of trees peeking out above it. *There must be a valley down there.* Thinking that Polly must've wandered off, he cursed under his breath and picked up a narrow deer trail through the purple heather that led in that direction. By the time he'd breached the ridge and peered down into the small valley where a bubbling burn weaved its way through the copse, his boots and the bottom of his trousers were soggy and caked with mud. Cupping his hands around his mouth he shouted.

"Polly? Where are you?" Nothing. "Polly Gunn, you answer me this instant!"

A flash of white caught his eye. *There!* Through the trees and across the burn. He'd just set off at a determined pace, speculating on which form of punishment would best befit the incorrigible little rapscallion, when his senses detected another presence ahead. It stopped him dead in his tracks. It wasn't human.

He closed his eyes, the rain battering his face, and focused on this new energy. It was animal... but there was something else. He couldn't work it out. He reached out to connect with Polly's energy and found it. She was not afraid; she was curious.

"Blast it all, if she's gone and trotted off after some bloody deer," he muttered irritably and stomped down the bank towards the burn. There was a narrow spot crossed with a spattering of small rounded boulders; they made perfect stepping stones. As he made his way across, his anger grew. Did the child not listen to anything he'd said? He'd specifically told her not to wander off, and now look what had happened. He was wet, cold and filthy, and in a foul mood.

"Polly Gunn. You're in a big heap of trouble, young lady! Do you hear me?"

A strange rumbling noise reverberated through the wood. *Was that a growl?*

"Polly?" he cried, concern peppering his tone. His senses prickled with alarm as the energy of whatever animal lay ahead changed from benign to malevolent in an instant.

He began to run, shouting his daughter's name in urgency. He focused on the girl's energy; she was scared now. His boots slipped on hidden rocks and tree roots as he ran. A hostile snarl came from his right. He turned on his heels and powered through thick brush and heather, tree branches whipping at his face. He called to the shadows, and they leapt to his command. Drawing on the dark as hard and fast as he could bear, for it was painful—like a thousand needles stabbing at his insides—he readied himself to attack whatever beast was threatening his daughter.

"Papa!" Polly's frightened scream tore through the air. "Papa!"

Midnight burst into a clearing, smoky tendrils of his power already flying from his fingers. Polly was sitting on the ground, her tiny face white with fear. She raised her good hand and pointed straight at him. His brow creased in confusion. *Where was the danger?*

A second too late, he realised he'd lost his focus on the malevolent energy and something with the weight of a small pony hit him from behind, knocking him flat to the floor.

He shot out his arms to break the fall but couldn't prevent his face from plunging into the leaf litter. Another scream came from Polly, and he sprang to his feet, spitting debris from his lips. Mud marred his vision, and he just caught sight of something large and shaggy bounding away from him through the wood.

The thing was fast; it had put a fair distance between them already. By the time he'd scrambled over to where Polly sat, crying and terrified, and he'd managed to wipe the majority of the grot from his face with his sleeve, it had disappeared.

Midnight fell to his knees beside the girl and scooped her towards him. She buried her face into his chest and sobbed while he frantically patted her down, checking for injuries. All desire to scold her dissipated as he discovered that she was intact, physically unharmed, but obviously and justifiably scared. Midnight held her to him, calming her tiny sobs, not realising how much time had passed until he heard the worried shouts of Bobby Mac in the distance.

He rose with Polly still in his arms and shouted to him. "Over here! I found her."

Midnight made his way through the trees towards the crossing at the burn to meet the driver, who, he was surprised and a little horrified to see, was accompanied by a very distressed and bedraggled-looking Agnes.

"Oh, my goodness! What on Earth happened?" Agnes picked up her pace as the soggy, mud-covered pair approached her. "We got worried when you didn't come straight back, and then we heard screaming."

"Ask Madam here," Midnight said. "On second thought, let's get back to the carriage and out of this blasted rain."

They all nodded in agreement and hurried back to the shelter of the carriage where Bobby Mac extracted another blanket from the box under the driver's seat and handed it to Midnight for the girl. Polly, teeth chattering, was attempting to explain the reason why she'd wandered so far away from the road in the first place.

"The tree wasn't big enough. I di... di'n't want to show me backside to the... the birds and bees. I only went a little further and when I was whizzin' I saw the w... wolf and went to say 'ello."

"There are no wolves in Scotland anymore, Polly," Agnes said in mild chastisement.

"I wouldn't be so sure about that, Miss Carmichael," Midnight said flatly. He was rubbing Polly down vigorously with the blanket. "Whatever creature I saw looked very wolf-like to me, although it's most likely a wild crossbreed of wolfhound or something," he added when Agnes's eyes widened further. He had a sudden vision of the bloodied corpse in a darkened alley in Edinburgh and shuddered. "Inspector Anderson said he thought a rabid dog was responsible for that attack in the city, and I'm inclined to agree. Although," he said with furrowed brow, "there must be more than one, as no dog could wander this far out in such a short time."

"Good heavens! Rabid dogs? Oh, Polly. You could've been killed, you naughty girl!" Agnes clutched her hand to her breast in shock.

"It's no' a dog, aye. It's the *Barghest*," Bobby Mac piped up dramatically. "There's been rumours of late that the moor-land beastie has been spotted again around these parts. Best not to go wandering off again, eh, miss?" He said this last part to Polly, who shook her head so violently her teeth chattered even harder.

"He wasn't going to eat me. Well, not at first, anyway. Papa scared him off."

"Hush now, child. We'll have no more talk of wolves and *Barghests*, whatever that means. You were very irresponsible to wander so far. Look what happens when you don't do as you're told," Agnes scolded.

Polly looked appealingly at her father, but he was focused on Bobby Mac. "What's a *Barghest*?"

"Stuff and nonsense is what it is," chided Agnes. "sir, I don't mean to be rude, but perhaps we should be on our way before we all catch our death? It's getting dark." She punctuated her meaning with a vigorous sneeze and a pleading look.

"The lady's right, sir. We've just time enough to reach Glenhaven an hour or so before dusk, if you please?"

Midnight looked the driver over who was sodden himself, even with his raincoat. He was right; their need to get to the cottage, settle in, and get warm was far greater than his need to know about the local folklore on beasties. The *Barghest* would have to wait.

3

SAMACH COTTAGE

The rain stopped as suddenly as it had started, and the sky turned from murky grey to a myriad of blue, pink, and orange. They pulled onto the road that led to the Glenhaven Estate as a choir of birds began their final chorus of the day. On the outer edge of the substantial estate, workers' cottages lay peppered here and there along the dirt track. It was a little past seven in the evening as they'd made good time with the clearing of the weather. It was a little while before sunset, yet Midnight noticed the tenants had already started shuttering their windows and locking away their livestock. He saw that several of the cottage doors had iron horseshoes hung on the lintels. One or two had strange symbols carved into the wood—probably Pictish in design, although he couldn't discern exactly. Superstition, it seemed, still played a part in the lives of the Scots.

Another fifteen minutes and the carriage pulled up outside a very appealing, two-story cottage with a thatched roof. Climbing roses clung to the stone walls at either side of the oak door upon which hung a sign that read 'Samach

Cottage'. Bobby Mac descended from his lofty seat and opened the carriage door for his dry but somewhat disheveled passengers. Midnight helped Polly out and was just offering his hand to Agnes when the cottage door flew open and Miss Carter came scurrying to greet them, a broad welcoming smile on her pretty face.

"Welcome, sir! Little miss... What the blazes?" She stopped short, the smile now gone and replaced with a look of concern at their state of dress.

Polly's usually neatly ringleted hair now hung in knotty strands, her pristine white dress stained brown with dirt. Midnight's boots and his entire frontage was filthy. Agnes climbed down, wrapped in a travelling blanket and looking dreadful, her red nose as bright as a brazier. Midnight, still holding the governess's hand, turned to face Miss Carter as she spoke. The housemaid looked the three of them up and down. He dropped Agnes's hand and reached up subconsciously to pick bits of leaf litter and twigs from his dark locks. Miss Carter was soon joined by Charlie who also stood open mouthed and gaping.

"Well," said Miss Carter, her lip twitching. "Glad to see you all made it in one piece."

Charlie wasn't even trying to hide his amusement and was openly grinning at them. "Blimey. Must be the first time I've ever felt overdressed," he said out of the corner of his mouth to Miss Carter.

Midnight cleared his throat.

"And poor Miss Carmichael, you look fit to drop." Miss Carter held out her arm towards Agnes and chivvied her inside. "And you, Miss Polly. Let's 'ave you. I've got everything ready and there's some hot soup on the range."

Midnight made to grab their overnight bags but Charlie stopped him. "I've got these, sir. You'll need to go inside and er... bathe sharpish." He struggled to smother his smile. "You're invited to dine at the big house in an hour."

"In an hour?" Midnight sighed heavily. After today, he really did not feel like being sociable. "I won't be able to get cleaned up in time," he said, gesturing at himself.

Charlie pushed open the door to the cottage with his shoulder and struggled through with the bags. "Not to worry. Me and Miss Carter will get you sorted. Miss Carmichael and the little miss are invited too."

"I'll need hot water for a quick bath. Is there one?"

"A bath? Yes. Probably not what you're used to at 'ome though. It's a bit more, um... public, you could say."

They came through the door into a narrow hallway with low ceilings. Charlie dropped the bags by the foot of the stairs and took his master through to the cosy kitchen where a small range threw off some significant heat. The smell of tomato soup permeated the air. His stomach rumbled in response. Miss Carter was by the range, hurriedly stripping Polly of her ruined clothes. She had stoked up the fire and put two big pots of water on to boil, ready to pour into the small tin bath that stood on the stone tiled floor by the range.

"*That* is the bath?" Midnight asked, incredulous. "But how...?" He'd been about to ask how he was supposed to fit *in* the minute receptacle and maintain his modesty and privacy at the same time, but Miss Carter preempted him.

"There's a screen, sir. See?" She stopped undressing Polly and nodded towards Charlie who obligingly went to the side of the inglenook fireplace and hauled out a three-panelled wooden screen decorated in a muted floral design. "We can all go sit in the parlour while you bathe." Her cheeks reddened as she spoke, she bit her top lip and cast her eyes sideways.

Midnight cleared his throat suddenly aware of several pairs of eyes on him and the fact they were listening to a discussion about him bathing. "The, um, soup smells delicious. Perhaps we could all have a small bowl to warm us up? I'm sure Miss Carmichael would appreciate some; she's feeling rather unwell," he said.

Miss Carter continued to fuss over Polly but answered him. "If Charlie will take your things upstairs, I'll see to the little miss and get you all some soup when she's washed. Miss Carmichael? If you're not feeling too poorly, would you mind fetching a clean gown and stockings for Miss Polly? I can air them out by the fire before she has to dress for dinner."

"Yes, of course," Miss Carmichael said. She rose from her chair, sneezed and went through to the hallway to find the required garments for Polly. Charlie followed her and began taking their bags upstairs leaving Midnight, Polly and Miss Carter alone. The girl was down to her shift and bare feet, and Miss Carter was attempting to heave one of the large pots of hot water from the stove top with a pair of folded linen strips.

Midnight stepped forward hurriedly and offered to take over. "Please, allow me?" He took the pot from her and poured it into the tin bath while she picked up a wooden bucket of cold water and added it to the hot. She put the bucket down, rolled up her sleeve, and swirled her hand through the water. A stray curl slipped from under her cap, and Midnight resisted the sudden urge to reach out and tuck it back under. He was still holding the iron pot and contemplating the colour of her hair when she caught him staring at her.

"You can put the pot back on the stove if ya like, sir," she suggested a little shyly. "It'll need filling again ready for yourself. There's a well out the back for the water. I'll go get some fresh soon as I'm done with this."

"I'll go. You've enough to be going on with." He put the pot back on the stove and bent for the bucket

Sometimes it was easy to forget that he came from an entirely different social class to his staff. Midnight always endeavored to make his employees feel comfortable in his presence. Their roles were clear within the household, and yet the lines blurred so often and so seamlessly. But he liked it that way. He led a somewhat secluded life by necessity and having a good relationship with those members of his permanent household made him feel... secure. He trusted his staff emphatically. Giles especially had, over the years, become more of a fatherly figure and confidant than a butler and lately Midnight had noticed Giles was growing closer to Miss Carter and Charlie. Of course, he was sure that had as much to do with Polly's adoration of them both as anything, but it was impossible not to like the lovely housemaid. Her smile lit up the darkest room.

"That's most kind, thank you." Miss Carter smiled coyly, pulling the screen around herself and Polly. From behind the safety of the painted wood, turning to her charge, she winked. "In you get then, Miss Polly. A quick rinse and you'll be as right as rain, eh?" Polly's shift appeared over the top of the screen, and Midnight heard the water swirling as his daughter stepped in and sat down.

As Midnight reached the rear door that led out from the kitchen into the rear garden, Miss Carter shouted after him. "Oh, and sir? Watch out for the rooster; he's the Devil." He thought he heard a giggle from behind the screen but couldn't tell if it had come from Polly or his housemaid.

The air was fresh compared to the muggy heat of the kitchen. He stood still for a second and breathed it in. There was something about the air in Scotland that cleansed the lungs and fed the soul. He spotted the well about fifteen feet from the cottage. A walled circle of reddish stone with a weather-worn windlass and peaked roof were highlighted by the orange glow of the slowly setting sun.

Atop the roof of the well stood a large cockerel, pausing his evening strut only to preen his gleaming red feathers. Midnight eyed the creature as he approached. The bird spotted Midnight and stood tall, stretching his neck high, pinning him with his beady eyes. The cockerel clucked in annoyance.

"Shoo!" Midnight said in response and waved the wooden bucket at him.

The big bird fluffed out his feathers, jumped off the roof and strutted off indignantly to stand a few feet away, clucking his disapproval at him.

Midnight pulled the hook and rope from the windlass and attached the bucket which he then let down into the water. He estimated the well to be about twenty feet deep judging by the time it took for the bucket to find water. He was halfway through winding it back up when the cockerel suddenly launched himself at Midnight's legs, spurs flying and wings beating. Midnight let go of the winding handle in surprise, and the bucket plummeted to the bottom with a resounding *splash*.

"Ah! Damn bird. Shoo!" He kicked at him, but the cockerel merely jumped back and then flew at him again. This time one of his spurs slashed through his trousers cutting Midnight's shin. "Ow! Why you blasted Devil. Away! Go on!" This time, hastily making sure no one was around to see, he shot a thin tendril of dark power at the rooster, hitting it square in the chest.

The bird was knocked backwards mid-hop and fell to

the ground panting heavily. For a moment Midnight thought the bird would die; he lay there, unmoving apart from the rapid rise and fall of his chest. But then he squawked, rolled over and skittered off, defeated.

Midnight rolled up his trouser leg to find a nasty gash in his shin. It was oozing blood steadily. He looked around. There wasn't much natural light left and, with no torches or candles to draw from, he would need to hurry in order to draw enough from the remaining daylight to heal himself. He took a deep breath, brushed some dirt from his leg and sent a thread of warm healing light from his palm to the injury. He watched as the bleeding stopped, and the wound began to close. It was almost healed when a shout from behind him made him jump and cease immediately. It was Agnes.

"Good grief, Lord Gunn! Are you all right?" She hurried over, holding her hands out to help him up off the ground.

He declined the offer with a quick wave of his hand and a kind smile. "No, no. Don't trouble yourself, dear Miss Carmichael. I'm fine."

"What on Earth happened to you? Oh, you're bleeding!" She fussed and clucked over him like a mother hen.

The rooster would probably be quite taken with her, he thought. "Really, I am perfectly fine. I just had a disagreement with the resident cock, that's all. He didn't take too kindly to me interrupting his evening display."

"Come inside, sir. I'll ask Charlie to come fetch the water. That wound will need tending to."

"It's just a scratch. Looks worse than it is, I assure you, Miss Carmichael. I am well and in no need of assistance. I can manage the water." He paused at the look on Agnes's face; she looked a little disappointed, he thought. Perhaps a suggestion to go and help Miss

Carter with Polly would sate her obvious desire to be helpful. He suggested as much, which merely earned him an abrupt 'If it pleases you, sir', and off she went. He shook his head. Women. He lived with four of them and didn't understand any of them—and probably never would.

He managed to retrieve a full bucket of water without incident this time, the cock being noticeably wary of him now. When he took it to the kitchen, Polly was already out of the bath and in a clean shift.

"That'll 'ave to do, I'm afraid, little miss. A quick wash got rid of the dirt but I ain't got a clue what I'm going to do with this tatty mess." Miss Carter tugged at Polly's tangled curls. "I ain't got time to set it again."

"There's some red ribbon in her vanity bag. Perhaps we can just tie it up out of the way?" Agnes suggested.

"Yeah, that could work, I suppose. Right then, Miss Polly, pop upstairs with Miss Carmichael and get dressed, eh? There's a good girl." Polly did as she was told and left with Agnes.

Two empty bowls of soup were on the table; Charlie had almost finished his, and there was a full one waiting for Midnight.

"Your soup's ready, sir. If you'd like to eat it while I prepare your bath." Miss Carter chirped.

Midnight thanked her and poured the well water into a hot iron pot, which hissed as he poured, steam rising to cover his face.

"Charlie? Be a love, and empty the bath, will ya? And fetch another bucket? His lordship can eat then while the pots are 'eating up."

Charlie gulped the remainder of his soup down, wiped his mouth, and went out the back with buckets of murky bathwater. They heard him tip the water away, and he returned with two full pails.

"Cheers, Charlie. Shouldn't take five minutes for these to 'eat up," she said, nodding towards the already simmering iron pans.

Midnight offered his assistance again, but Miss Carter shook her head, insistent this time. "No, thank you, sir. I can manage. You eat. I expect you're starvin'."

"I am, rather," he admitted. "A little tired too. I wish I didn't have to go up to the house this evening. I'm in no mood to socialise."

Miss Carter offered him a sympathetic smile as she wiped the ring of soap-scum from the edge of the bath. "It's manners, I expect, eh, sir? Being that you 'ave to go say hello to Ms. Adams n'all. I should think she'll have a grand dinner prepared and everything. Miss Polly is excited."

"She would be. Given her origins, she seems to have acquired a taste for fine dining rather quickly."

"Who could blame her, eh? We've all been spoiled by Mrs. Phillips's cooking. I ain't never had food so delicious since I came to live at Meriton House."

Midnight smiled warmly, picked up his bowl and a spoon, and began eating. Miss Carter cut a fresh slice of brown cob and buttered it. Handing it to him on a side plate, she said, "'Appen it's a good thing you'll be dining at Glenhaven a lot during our stay. I'm afraid my cooking ain't up to the standard of Mrs. Phillips." She giggled shyly.

"Absolute nonsense," he replied. "This soup is delicious." Had he been a little more astute and less exhausted, he would've noticed how his words made the colour rise in her cheeks and her eyes twinkle, but as it was, he found himself distracted by Charlie bringing back another load of water from the well.

"Pop it in the other pot for me, will ya', Charlie?" Miss Carter said.

Charlie did as he was instructed then turned to address his master. "I've already 'ung out your clothes for this evening, sir. I'll bring down the large sheet from the linen closet for after you've bathed."

"Much obliged, Charlie. Thank you." He realised with horror that he'd have to make his way upstairs after he'd bathed, damp, and wearing nothing but a sheet. He truly hoped that the women folk *did* stay hidden in the front parlour. Had he known about the lack of a private bathroom, he might have reconsidered their accommodation before embarking upon this trip. Still, his cousin had been very generous in offering him the cottage. Ms. Adams had at first offered for him and his party to stay with her at the big house, but Midnight liked his privacy too much to accept that, and so had settled on the cottage instead. It seemed ironic that for one who valued privacy, he was about to take a very public bath—screen or no screen.

When the bath was ready, Miss Carter discreetly left the kitchen to go upstairs and see if Polly and Agnes needed anything. Charlie stayed behind to assist Midnight. As his valet for the duration of the trip, Charlie was taking much pride in his new, if temporary, position and trying his best to remember the training that Giles had given him. He waited patiently at the kitchen table while his master sank into the welcome water, knees bent upwards in order to accommodate his length. The water stung the partially healed wound where the affronted bird had slashed him. Now that Agnes was safely out of the way and he was out of sight behind the screen, he healed it fully, leaving behind the barest pink line in place of the cut. Miss Carter had placed a bar of soap and a jug of warm water on a stool next to the bath with which to wash his hair. He tipped the contents of the jug over his head and scrubbed vigorously trying to remove any trace of mud and leaves from his body. The soap was lavender scented, a little too feminine for his taste. He wondered who had provided the soap? Miss Carter, Miss Carmichael, or his host, Felicity Adams? He would have to remember to buy a more appropriately fragranced soap at the next opportunity. In the meantime, he hoped he'd remembered to pack his cologne. The crackle of the fire, the warm water, and the lull of the early evening pulled him into a state of relaxation that was all too short lived.

"Begging your pardon, sir, but you're meant to be up at the 'ouse in twenty minutes. Shall I fetch the bath sheet?" Charlie said.

"Already? But I've barely had time to wash."

"It's a good walk to the big 'ouse, mind."

Midnight sighed heavily but resigned himself to leaving his watery sanctuary much earlier than he would've liked. "Fine. Hand me the sheet, Charlie." He rose and swiped his hands over his hair and down his body to slough off most of the water. A moment later, Charlie appeared holding up a large bath sheet, which Midnight took and wrapped around himself. He stepped out of the bath and stood by the fire to quickly dry himself. When he was dry, he slipped his feet into his soft leather loafers which had been warming by the hearth. Moving quickly and covertly out of the kitchen and following Charlie upstairs without encountering any of the women, Midnight was surprised to find his heart was pounding by the time he made it safely into his room.

Christ! Things were much simpler when I only had myself to worry about, he thought.

He'd spent much of his adult life alone since his father, Josiah Gunn, died when he was just fifteen; his mother,

Josephine, had died giving birth to him. Since his father's untimely passing, it had been just Midnight, Giles and Mrs. P. for the longest time. And then Polly had come along, and now his household seemed to be expanding at an alarming rate.

Not one for mingling, due to the fact that he hid a dark and terrible secret, he'd had a lot of trouble adjusting to the amount of bodies now living in his private home. Indeed, he was still adjusting to it. The very fact that he must don his best suit and go and postulate as the perfect dinner guest filled him with dread. For although he now had full control over his powers, he was always wary around company. Even those around him who knew his secret never spoke of it, except for Polly and only when they were alone. She knew it was not a subject to ever be discussed in public.

Ten minutes later, he was dressed in his best, his hair still wet but neatly slicked back, and he was downstairs waiting for Polly and Agnes to join him.

He was pacing in the front parlour, checking his pocket watch, when they both walked in through the door. Polly, in a clean blue dress, white stockings, cleaned shoes, and lace shawl, looked very pretty, her curly mass neatly tied back with a red ribbon. Agnes Carmichael surprised him in a comely but demure evening gown of purple taffeta with matching shoulder wrap. She'd powdered her face and applied some rouge and lip stain but her red-rimmed eyes and swollen nose betrayed her attempt to hide her cold.

"Miss Carmichael, are you sure you want to go this evening? If you're feeling unwell..."

"I'm fine. Thank you, my lord," she interjected. Her voice had taken on a distinctly muffled quality, and she sniffed loudly.

"Very well, then. I suppose we had better go. It wouldn't

do to be late the first evening, now would it?" He offered his arm to the governess who took it gratefully, looking like she needed the support. Polly skipped along beside them as they took the lengthy path from Samach cottage to Glenhaven House.

Midnight watched as his daughter frolicked ahead, completely carefree and unfazed by the earlier events of this afternoon. As they walked, he remembered the size and shape of the beast in the woods. He'd had but a fleeting glimpse of it but it was enough to send a chill down his spine thinking of what could have happened to Polly. She had been adamant it had meant her no harm, but she hadn't sensed the malice and fear rolling off of the creature. Midnight had, and he knew that thing was a killer.

There was movement near the tree line to the side of the path and his head whipped around, alert. He caught sight of the white bobtail of a wild rabbit bounding off to the safety of the trees, and he exhaled in relief.

"Come here, sweetheart," Midnight called to Polly. "Hold Miss Carter's hand. She is chilled and needs our help."

The girl stopped skipping ahead and came trotting back towards them eager to assist her dear Papa and her beloved governess. He didn't know why, but he had the strongest need to keep Polly close to him tonight. As a gentle breeze tickled the very tops of the branches in the nearby trees, it felt as if the entire wood was watching him... and waiting.

4

GLENHAVEN

As they neared Glenhaven House, Midnight was able to appreciate that it must've been a very imposing building once. The date within the engraved coat of arms above the grand entrance read '1735'. The house, originally built in the Palladian style, had acquired elements of neoclassical architecture as the years passed. As a result, the façade was as majestic as it was eclectic. Dual stone staircases to the right and left led to tall stone pillars which supported the triangular roof that protected the front door. One might be fooled into thinking it was an ancient Greek temple had it not been for the intricately carved and distinctly Scottish thistles that wound their way around the base of the columns and up the sides of the stone door arch. As grand as it looked from a distance, there were signs of neglect beginning to show.

Midnight thought about what Bobby Mac had told him of his mistress having to sell many of the horses after her husband had died, and he wondered just how his cousin was managing to stay afloat these days. He knew what it was to be alone and to manage a great estate. Ms. Adams must be quite a capable woman if she was running this place by herself. She wasn't much older than himself. She had neither children nor had she married again, although perhaps it was a little too soon for that.

"Can I ring it? Please, Papa?" Polly pointed excitedly at the metal bell pull. Midnight nodded, and she grabbed the brass handle, yanking it hard.

They heard the bell ringing within, and it was a few minutes later that the door was opened by neither a maid nor butler but by a woman. She was elegantly dressed for the evening, her hair perfectly coiffed and her shining face delicately made up.

"Cousin? Oh, how delightful! Do come in." Ms. Felicity Adams stepped aside to allow her guests entry. She fixed them all with a beaming smile, but she could not hide her nerves from Midnight. He could sense emotions, and his cousin's outward confidence contradicted her inner feelings.

"Good evening, Ms. Adams." Midnight replied, deeming the formal greeting more appropriate since he barely remembered his distant relative. Once they were all inside and Ms. Adams had closed the door, Midnight introduced everyone. "Ms. Adams, please allow me to present my daughter, Polly, and her governess, Miss Agnes Carmichael." Polly stuck out her left arm, the one that ended in a stump.

"Pleased to make your 'quaintence, Ms. Adams."

Their host's mask slipped for the merest second, then she gathered herself, took hold of Polly's arm, and shook it politely.

"Very pleased to meet you, Miss Polly."

Midnight smiled as Polly nodded in satisfaction—it seemed Ms. Adams had passed her test.

"And you, Miss Carmichael, welcome, welcome." The two women shook hands, and their host directed them all through the wide entrance hall into a pleasant little drawing room.

"I thought we could have a glass of sherry while we wait for dinner? You must all be so very tired. Mr. MacDonald informs me you had a minor incident on your journey here? I do hope you are all recovered."

"Yes, thank you. It certainly was an eventful journey. Sherry sounds delightful." It didn't. Midnight hated sherry. But in the interest of good manners, he accepted a small glass. Miss Carmichael stifled a sneeze, which made it sound more like a snort, which in turn, made Polly giggle. Miss Carmichael blushed.

"Why, you don't sound well at all, dear lady. Do you have a cold? Come, sit by the fire. I'll have Craigson fetch you a warmed brandy. It should help."

"Oh, but I don't wish to be any trouble. Really. I'm quite all right," the governess said but didn't protest further at being ushered to a seat by the roaring fire.

"Craigson?" Ms. Adams called and a moment later a young man in a footman's livery entered the room. Midnight wondered why the fellow hadn't opened the door for them earlier. "Oh, Craigson. Would you be a darling and fetch poor Miss Carmichael a warm brandy?"

"Aye, ma'am. Right away." The fellow gave a perfunctory nod and left.

"You must tell me what happened during your journey. MacDonald tells me there's a 'beastie' of sorts on the loose."

"Ah! Yes, well, I'm not sure what it was really—probably a stray dog. But it'll no doubt be miles away by now." Midnight tried to downplay the incident, not wanting to frighten Polly.

"Let us hope so. If it happens to wander too near Glenhaven, I'm sure Faolan and Artair will see it off. Those are

my dogs," Ms. Adams explained. "Irish Wolfhounds—
nothing much scares them. I keep them for protection, you
see."

"Is there much you need protecting from, Ms. Adams?"
Midnight raised an eyebrow, and she giggled.

"Dearest cousin, I am a widow who lives alone, and I am
the sole heir to my husband's estate. I would say there is
much I need protecting from, wouldn't you? However,
nothing of the four-legged kind." She flashed him a coy
smile and batted her eyelashes.

Midnight shifted uncomfortably in his seat, his senses
picking up a sudden wave of desire from her. The bell rang
for dinner, and his relief was palpable. How he wished he
could be back in the cottage, eating soup, and listening to
Polly read–or even better, be back at Meriton House in
London and chatting over a brandy with Giles.

Never comfortable playing the role of a socialite,
Midnight was usually only forced to integrate with
members of his own class for business. He much preferred
the rustic taverns and the anonymity of the city and its
parks at night for those times when the walls of Meriton—
his London home—became monotonous. However, for
Polly's sake, he recognised the necessity to venture into
polite society on the odd occasion. It did not do for any
young woman in London to be hidden away; one day she
would be heir to the Gunn fortune, and Midnight intended
that she knew exactly what she was getting into.

Polly was special, too; like him, she had certain abilities.
She was able to see auras. He had discovered this after she
had come to stay at Meriton. Her talent had made her a
target for Hemlock Nightingale, as had Midnight's own
powers. His unique abilities had been the reason his father
had kept him away from polite society for most of his life, a

habit that Midnight had continued right up until the little girl had become a permanent addition to his family.

Josiah Gunn had taught his son at home, he'd never had a governess; his father had been too worried that Midnight might hurt someone should his then uncontrollable powers accidentally manifest. Midnight never went to university either; he'd continued to further his studies at Meriton. Josiah had collected an impressive range of books for the family library, including many on the occult which had become a particular area of expertise for both himself and his son. In a way, Midnight had resented his powers as a child, but as he'd grown and had realised their uses for the greater good, he'd become accustomed to them and had now learned to master them.

As much as he hated the company of his peers, he realised that Polly, being of low birth *and* an amputee, would struggle being raised in as isolated a way as he had. Her ability to see people's 'colours', as she liked to call them, wasn't as restrictive as his, and so she was allocated a governess and would, in time, be introduced to society in preparation for her future as a wealthy heiress. The self-imposed solitude that had been his haven was slowly being stripped away, and he wasn't sure how he felt about that yet.

The Glenhaven table seated twenty-four and was housed by a dining room dripping with aged opulence. Much like the exterior, it oozed grandeur, but upon second glance, the faded drapes, peeling wallpaper, and flaking gold gilt hinted at neglect. The four of them—himself, Polly, Miss Carmichael, and their host—looked lost, sitting at one end of the long, polished walnut table. Conversation resumed once they were settled and Craigson had filled their wine glasses and their bowls. The first course, Midnight was not enthused to see, was a thin chicken broth accompanied by warm dinner rolls. He would gladly have forsaken this starter and gone straight for the main course. He noted the lack of any housemaids or extra footmen and again found himself wondering if his cousin had fallen on hard times. For himself, he kept minimal staff because there was only him and Polly to look after, and he liked his privacy. Perhaps his cousin was the same.

"Forgive my impertinence, Ms. Adams, but I notice you keep a minimal staff... much like myself," he added, for fear his statement might appear rude.

Ms. Adams did not reply immediately. She finished the soup on her spoon, put the cutlery down, and picked up her napkin and dabbed her mouth gently. Clearing her throat and fixing him with an indulgent smile, she replied. "Firstly, if we are to be neighbours for the whole summer, cousin. I must insist you call me Felicity or cousin. Either will suffice. We are kin after all, albeit distant, yes?" She tilted her head questioningly, and Midnight nodded in return. "Secondly, you are correct, of course. My staff is very much reduced since my late husband's passing. Poor, dear George." She paused for dramatic effect.

Midnight could sense no genuine sense of grief from her; she clearly hadn't loved her husband.

"We *are* family." She paused again, contemplating. "And I feel I can trust you with the truth of it."

Miss Carmichael, who had until now been concentrating hard on her chicken soup, perked up at the potential gossip.

"You see, my dear George was a terrible gambler. It wasn't until his passing that I discovered how much money he owed. As a result, I have been forced to sell many of our possessions and let the majority of my staff go to compensate." She made a small sound like a hiccup and pressed the back of her hand to her mouth as if stifling a sob.

Her grief at the loss of her treasured possessions and social status *was* genuine. Midnight could see that. Ms. Adams distress and unfortunate circumstance caused Miss Carmichael to gasp in horror. "Oh, Ms. Adams. You poor, poor thing. How perfectly dreadful. Why, you must not know *where* to turn? It is a good thing that we came, I think. You shall have some company and a sympathetic ear at the very least." Miss Carmichael's gushing commiserations, coupled with Polly's sudden extraction from her chair to go and fling her arms around their despairing host, fair sent Felicity into a pitiful, and slightly awkward, bout of the vapours.

Midnight managed to suppress the wry smirk that threatened his otherwise sympathetic outward appearance enough to summon Craigson and instruct him to fetch smelling salts as quickly as possible. He reminded himself not to be too judgmental of his cousin. Not many women of breeding ever married for love. Marriages were matches made for the benefit of both the families involved. Even if Ms. Adams felt little grief for her late husband, it was clear she now found herself in dire circumstances and needed help to re-establish herself. He may not be a willing socialite, but he was well connected in the business world- perhaps he could persuade a lawyer or accountant to look over her affairs. He made up his mind to suggest the idea once she had calmed herself and they could talk in private.

"How are you finding life in the British Isles, Miss Carmichael? I imagine it is quite different to what you are used to."

Agnes beamed at the attention their hostess lay upon her and answered eagerly. "Oh, yes, Ms. Adams. Father used to hold many parties at the house. It was always full of music and chatter. Life's a little quieter here, I suppose." She smiled and dipped a shoulder Midnight cleared his throat. "—though I am a governess, so one shouldn't expect it to be all fun and parties." She rushed on, conscious of how her words might have been misconstrued.

Ms. Adams raised a quizzical eyebrow. "Indeed not. But you know the saying—'All work and no play, makes Jack a dull boy.'" Felicity turned her eyes to Midnight. "Cousin?"

"Yes, Ms. Adams?"

"Miss Carmichael is far too pretty to be a dull Jack, is she not?" she asked teasingly.

Agnes blushed, suddenly very interested in the food on her plate.

"Do you not keep good entertainment at Meriton? Am I going to be forced to hold a ball in your honor?"

"Ooo!" squeaked Polly.

Midnight put down his fork, took a measured sip of his wine, and gave his cousin a placatory smile. "In truth, I find balls extremely dull, the music too loud, and the guests too much fueled by drink and idle gossip to be stimulating. I much prefer intimate dinners, such as this one, where I can sufficiently appreciate the good company and provocative conversation."

Felicity cocked her head slightly, contemplating his reply. She reached her gloved hand across the table and laid it to rest upon his own. "There is merit in what you say, dear cousin. I, myself, am partial to *intimate* dinners. It is so hard to really get to know a person over the noise and pace of a ball," she cooed.

Midnight removed his hand from her grasp and went for his wine glass.

Felicity took the hint and retreated. "Although balls do

have their place, of course. They allow us ladies to let down our hair, show off our dresses, and indulge in as much idle gossip as we please without the fear of reproach. You'd be amazed at what secrets one can discover at such gatherings, cousin." She dabbed her mouth again and eyed him from underneath her long, upturned lashes.

"I ain't never been to a ball, Papa." Polly piped up, her enthusiasm spilling out.

"I'm afraid I will be too busy to attend any such gathering, sweetheart. I am here on business after all. Perhaps I am the dull Jack on this occasion."

"Hmpf." Polly's face fell in disappointment, as did Agnes'. Felicity merely smiled.

The rest of the dinner progressed without any further incident of drama or subsequent swooning, much to Midnight's relief. Polly began to yawn during the dessert course, and Midnight saw the need to impress upon his host who was getting along great guns with his governess that perhaps it was time they retire. It had been a very long day and he wanted to make an early start in the morning.

"Oh, goodness me!" Ms. Adams exclaimed. "Have I really kept you all this long? How very rude of me. I blame you all entirely, of course. It's not often I am privileged to such entertaining company these days."

"I am happy to have been of service to you then, madame." Midnight smiled. "But it appears we *must* ask your leave or I fear I will be forced to carry both Polly *and* Miss Carmichael back to the cottage."

The unintentional outrageousness of this statement elicited shocked giggles from Polly and Ms. Adams. Miss Carmichael, however, merely flushed beetroot and looked intently at her wine glass.

"My dear cousin, you will have us all in a tizzy I am sure.

'Dull Jack' indeed!" Ms. Adams tutted. "But wait. Before you take your leave, I have something for you. Craigson? Bring me the papers." Her footman nodded and left the room. "Cousin. I ask your forgiveness if I've been a little presumptuous, *but* when you said in your letter that you were here looking for property, I took it upon myself to do a little digging of my own. I've prepared a list of properties for you that may suit. Being somewhat of a local, I do know the best areas and, well... You will see. Here's Craigson now." She took the folio from the footman and handed it to Midnight, who took it with genuine appreciation.

"Thank you, Ms. Adams. I am very grateful. I will take a look later this evening and add your list to my own after I have seen Polly to bed. As I said, we have an early start in the morning, but I do thank you for your hospitality. It was a very enjoyable evening."

"You are most welcome, cousin. And *do* call me Felicity. I absolutely insist on it. Now, off you all go and leave me *all alone!*" She swept her arm dramatically as she rose from the table then escorted them out of the dining room and into the entrance hall where they exchanged pleasantries and goodbyes.

Once outside, Midnight drew in a deep cleansing breath. After nearly three hours of polite conversation, he longed for the isolation of his bedroom at the cottage. His shoulders ached and his collar felt too tight, but he still managed to scoop up his daughter and carry her home. Polly was asleep by the time they arrived. Miss Carmichael went straight upstairs and did not emerge again. Coughing and intermittent sneezes could be heard coming from her room. Midnight carried Polly upstairs and put her straight to bed, removing her shoes and coat but not bothering to remove her evening clothes for fear of waking her.

"Good night, Miss Peeps. Sleep tight," he whispered and kissed her little upturned nose. As he stepped out of her room and closed the door, he heard a dreadful commotion from somewhere outside of the house.

Miss Carter was still awake and was in the kitchen, banking up the fire for the night when he walked in. "Evenin', sir. Was it Charlie you're wanting? Only he's out back. We heard a right old racket. Sounded like—"

She didn't get chance to finish before Midnight shot out of the door and into the dark. His senses had picked up a threat, and if Charlie was outside, he needed to be there too. Aside from the barest of orange glows from the kitchen window, the rear garden was pitch black. Had there been a clear sky and a full moon, he would've been able to see, but as it was, the sky had clouded over. He focused on the threat: it was animal, and it was on the hunt.

"Charlie?" he called. The shadows twitched, waiting to be called. "Where are you?" Midnight's voice seemed flat and lost in the vast dark. A lone owl hooted somewhere in the distance, carried to a fade by the evening breeze. He called out again, and to his relief, he received an answer.

"Over 'ere, sir," came an urgent whisper ahead of him.

Midnight turned himself in the direction of Charlie's voice. He still sensed the animal, but it seemed less focused on its hunt now and more wary. He searched for Charlie amongst the shadows, his careful footsteps crunching ominously on the gravel path. He found him crouched behind the well, peering into the thick bushes ahead.

"What is it?" Midnight asked.

"I dunno, sir. Something's out there, prowlin'. Whatever it is, I think it's waitin' for something. Do you feel anythin'?"

"I did. But it's changed. In the house, I felt nothing but threat. Now, it is as you say; it's waiting."

"What for?"

"I don't know."

He opened his mind and let his senses drift, probing the foliage ahead for the intruding energy. When he found it, his skin prickled, similar to the way it did when he accepted the shadows but alarmingly more inviting. The energy nudged back, and he could feel a certain sense of curiosity within it, a need to communicate almost. *What are you doing, beastie?* He thought. And then he knew. The animal was waiting for *him*. He was sure of it, he could only explain it as a fleeting connection of minds between himself and the animal. But why was it focusing on him? That was a conundrum he could not solve without further investigation. Should he risk an approach? Would any action put Charlie in danger? The others were safe in the cottage, but what if one of them came outside, could he protect them all if the creature decided to attack? He strained to see in the dark, he didn't even know what sort of animal it was. He probed again but felt nothing.

"It's gone," he said to Charlie. "Probably just a curious fox. Let's go inside."

Charlie looked dubious but didn't need any convincing to retreat.

Midnight stayed a few moments, testing the air just to make sure he was alone. That energy had an air of familiarity about it, and he suddenly felt very vulnerable, but he couldn't quite determine why.

5

MURDER MOST FOUL

Midnight slept poorly. He'd been on alert all through the night since the incident in the garden. He and Charlie had waited, crouched behind the well, for a good while until Midnight felt the animal fade into the distance. They didn't discover the reason for the nighttime visit until morning.

"Bleedin' 'ell, Charlie!" Miss Carter yelled as Charlie dangled the dead cockerel in front of her shocked face. She jumped back from the kitchen table where she was preparing breakfast. "What did you do that for?" she demanded.

"I guess it was a fox what got 'im last night," he surmised, still waggling the limp corpse.

"What's that I hear?" said Midnight, who had just entered the kitchen already dressed and ready for the day.

"You were right, sir. Sommin' killed the cock."

"Saved me a job," Midnight muttered, remembering the demon-bird's spur in his shin. "See, I told you it was likely a fox." That wasn't the impression he'd gotten at all. The animal he'd sensed had seemed intent on its purpose; he was sure it had been waiting for him as if it had caused the commotion deliberately to lure him outside.

But then, if that was the case, why had it not attacked? What was its motive? Just to observe? He supposed it *might* have been a fox if his senses were off, but that was unlikely. No, this animal was far more sentient than a fox, and foxes bite the heads off their prey. The cockerel was whole. It was puzzling indeed.

"Where did you find it?" he asked Charlie.

"Well, that's the funny fing, i'nit. It was on the back step. Laid there all nice 'n neat, like a bleedin' present!" Charlie huffed.

Or a message, Midnight mused. Wasn't there some mythology connected to dead birds and warnings?

"Hang it in the pantry, Charlie. Might as well pluck it and cook it, eh? Never look a gift 'orse in the mouth, is what my old mum would say." Miss Carter seemed jovial this morning.

Midnight watched her as she went about the business of preparing breakfast for them all. A few loose curls had worked their way out from under her cap again. They bobbed and swayed along with her movements. The morning sun glinted softly off her skin, highlighting the sprinkling of freckles on the bridge of her nose. She was laughing and chatting with Charlie as she worked. Midnight found himself mesmerised. Her gaze shifted, and just for a second, met his own and held it. His stomach lurched, causing him to take in an involuntary breath. She smiled at him, no— *for* him, which caused his heart to thump hard against his ribcage. Her smile lasted only a second but felt like a minute, so that when she looked away and carried on chatting with Charlie, it left him cold and confused with the loss of it. He shook off the feeling.

"Miss Adams has kindly offered us her carriage today, Charlie. I'd appreciate it if you would go up to the stables and help Bobby Mac prepare it. He has some new harness or other that allows for greater control of the horses. I thought you could take a look at it and see what you think? If you approve, we might get one for home," Midnight said. He knew how eager Charlie was to learn. If Miss Carter could spare him for the day, he would invite him along for the drive.

"Yes, sir. I'll go right after breakfast, then," he said, his eyes bright.

Polly came down, dressed in her day clothes but without her governess. "Good morning, Papa," she said in a sleepy but very proper voice. It made Midnight smile. She was trying so hard with her elocution lessons. "Morning, everyone." She made her way to Midnight who held open his arms to her.

"Good morning, sweetheart." He hugged her and tugged her curls. "Are you ready for our trip? Where's Miss Carmichael?"

"Oh, Aggie ain't feeling well. I don't think she's comin'," Polly said, yawning. "What's for breakfast?"

"Poor lamb. I'll take her up somethin' in a bit. For you, little miss." Miss Carter placed a bowl of hot porridge adorned with stewed apple and honey on the table in front of Polly.

"Ah. That is unfortunate. I was hoping Miss Carmichael would keep this little scallywag from under my feet today while we're house hunting." He winked at his daughter.

"I can still come, can't I? Please don't make me stay 'ome," Polly pleaded.

"As long as you behave and promise *not* to wander off again," he said in a stern manner. He meant it too. The beast in the woods and the incident last night had unnerved him. They would be visiting two properties in the area today, which presented the minx with plenty of opportunity to get into trouble.

"I promise! Really, I do." She nodded so emphatically it was comical.

"Then we have a deal, Polly Peeps, and deals cannot be broken." Midnight addressed Charlie next. "Would you like to come along for the ride, Charlie? Providing Miss Carter can spare you, of course?"

Charlie looked at Miss Carter who nodded. "I'll have my hands full, I'm sure. But I'll get along nicely without anyone 'ere getting under *my* feet. Long as you bring us a bucket of fresh water in before you go, eh?"

"I'll see to it now, then I'll go to the stables." Charlie said. He wiped his mouth on the back of his hand, rose from the table and went to carry out his morning tasks.

Midnight was looking through the details of the first property they were visiting. It was a place called Hooley House and it sat at the foot of the Pentland Hills, south of Edinburgh. He estimated it would take them about an hour and a half by carriage from Samach Cottage.

"I forgot to tell you, sir. There's a newspaper in the hall for you. You can take it on your journey; somethin' to read."

"Thank you, Miss Carter. I think I might have a look at it now, though. I still have time before the carriage is ready."

"As you like, sir. It's just on the hall table by the brolly stand."

Midnight made his way to the hall table. The newspaper was folded and waiting on a china plate next to a vase with freshly picked flowers and—

He froze. The hair on his arms prickled with the sudden ice-cold fear that spread through his veins. *Hemlock!* He stood, frozen to the spot with his hand halfway reaching for the newspaper. The wildflowers and heather had been prettily arranged in the vase, interspersed with copious sprigs of deadly hemlock.

"Miss Carter?" he called, trying hard to keep the fear and fury from his voice. "Can you come here, please?"

There was a pattering of hurried footsteps on the stone floor as she came to see what he wanted. "Can you not find it, sir? It's right there on the—" She stopped when she saw his face, thin lipped and white. "S... sir?"

"Who put those flowers there?" he pointed at the offending items.

"I did," she replied in a quiet voice.

"Yes, but *who* brought them? Where did they come from?"

"No one. I picked 'em meself f... from out the garden. I just thought they'd brighten the place up a bit." She paused and pulled at her bottom lip with her teeth. "I'm sorry," she muttered, her eyes glistening.

Midnight let out a breath. However, the relief he felt that it was merely an oversight on his housemaid's part was short lived. "Do you know what this plant is?" He pointed to the plant with the long straight stems, fern-like leaves, and clusters of tiny white blooms. Miss Carter shook her head. "It is hemlock." He saw her eyes widen. "And it is *deadly*." She gasped aloud at this. Her hand flew to cover her mouth. "If Polly had touched it and gotten sap on her hands and then in her mouth, she could have *died*, Miss Carter. How could you be so careless?" He immediately regretted his tone as the poor girl spluttered and burst into tears.

"Oh, sir. I'm so sorry. Truly I am. I 'ad no idea." Her shoulders were heaving now, her words uttered in between sobs. "I just thought they looked pretty. I would... would *never*—" She broke off to dig for a handkerchief in her apron pocket but came up short.

Midnight, now feeling terribly guilty, offered her his. She took it and blew with one hand while Midnight took her other. "Miss Carter. It is I who should apologise. I did not mean to upset you. It was just that seeing *that* particular plant in our house. It made me think... of *him*." He patted her hand trying to soothe her but at the mention of the deplorable villain that had once ripped her soul from her body, a fresh wave of sobbing began. Midnight stood there, totally out of his depth and not knowing what to do next.

Polly came hurtling through from the kitchen to investigate all the noise. Her face dropped as she caught sight of her beloved Miss Carter in such a state of distress. She pinned her father with such a scowl he actually took a step back. Polly faced him with her arms folded, tapping one foot impatiently on the floor, and a look of angry expectation on her face. Midnight did the only thing he could think of doing and impulsively wrapped his housemaid up in his arms, holding her to him and gently patting her back. It was what he did with Polly when she was upset. He just hoped it worked on older females.

Charlie chose that exact moment to open the front door to announce the arrival of the carriage. He took one look at the carnage and stepped deftly back outside, closing the door behind him.

Blast it all! Midnight thought. *Will we ever be rid of Hemlock-bloody-Nightingale?* Although, on second thought, he toyed with the notion that dealing with a soul-stealing, demonically possessed ex-doctor was, in fact, easier than dealing with an hysterical housemaid.

There was a knock on the door and Charlie called from outside. "Um... carriage is here, sir."

"We'll be right out, Charlie." Polly yelled back.

Miss Carter's sobs subsided enough for Midnight to let her go. His jacket's lapel was wet with her tears, and he mourned the sudden loss of her closeness, so much so that he almost stepped forward to envelop her again. He cleared his throat. "The flowers are very nice. As was the thought behind them. Once again, I apologise for my abrupt manner. You understand why, of course?"

There was a moment of awkward silence between them until Polly piped up and reminded them of the awaiting carriage.

Miss Carter bobbed a slight curtsey and said, "A misunderstanding is all, sir. I'll get rid of them straight away." She did not meet his eyes but took the vase and its contents away.

Polly thrust his overcoat into his hands, huffed at him, and stomped out the door, leaving Midnight alone and wondering yet again just how and why he'd allowed himself to become surrounded by a household full of women.

6

SENSE AND SENSIBILITY

"Cousin! Good morning," Ms. Adams called from the carriage. "I hope you don't mind, but you'll be giving me a lift to the city. I have business." She beamed.

Polly waved at her and skipped up to the carriage.

"Not at all, cousin," Midnight replied. Not yet content to call her Felicity, he compromised in using the same semi-polite but all-too familial term that she used to address him.

Bobby Mac opened the carriage door and Polly and Midnight climbed inside.

"Edinburgh is further than Hooley House, is it not?" Midnight enquired.

"It is. We shall drop you off at Hooley then Bobby shall take me into the city and come back for you. I'll be away overnight. I apologise that I will not be able to invite you to dine tonight. Do forgive me? This was an unexpected... appointment."

"No apology is necessary. Business is business," Midnight said, although he had noticed her slight hesitation at describing her trip as an appointment. He wondered at the sudden urgency of it and if everything was all right. He would have asked, but he was not one to pry.

"Miss Carter's goin' to roast that rooster for dinner anyway," Polly said helpfully. "I reckon there'll be enough chicken for a banquet, he was a big bugg—"

"Thank you, Polly," Midnight interrupted.

"The rooster? From the cottage garden?" Ms. Adams frowned.

"Ah. Yes. He met with an unfortunate accident. I'm sorry," he said.

"Did he finally fall down the well?" Midnight could tell from his cousin's tone that she was not overly fond of the avian devil either and he felt somewhat more comfortable explaining that a fox had killed it. "Good riddance I say. The thing was a menace." She winked at Polly and said, "I hope for your sake he tastes better than he ever behaved." This made the girl giggle.

Midnight could tell his daughter liked Ms. Adams and that made him relax a little bit in her company. Much of the journey passed with bursts of polite conversation, interspersed by Polly's enthusiastic chattering. When the conversation petered out and Polly became content to sit and take in the scenery, Ms. Adams too fell quiet.

Midnight noticed the slight smile on her face as she absent-mindedly picked at a loose thread on her glove. She was lost in a far-off daydream, perhaps, remembering a happier time. *Or,* he thought, *perhaps thinking on one to come?* Yes, that was it, she was going to meet someone. He could feel the excitement emanating from her now, coupled with nerves. He wondered if she was going to meet a potential suitor. It was clearly someone she liked. That much he could tell. He smiled inwardly, hoping for her sake, the meeting was a fruitful one and that the potential suitor could make her happy. *Should I be that person?*

That thought was entirely unexpected and completely took him by surprise. He had never considered marriage before and wondered why it had suddenly entered his head now. Perhaps it was the need to provide a stable family environment for his daughter, or the immediate need of his cousin to regain her former status. Was he duty-bound to step in? *It would certainly kill two birds with one stone,* he thought. He considered Felicity Adams for a moment; she was handsome enough with her dark auburn hair, green eyes, and slender body. He wondered upon the milky smoothness of her skin, dappled with little constellations of tan freckles, and if her skin would feel as soft as it looked. He was suddenly very conscious of the rising blush in his cheeks and picked up the newspaper—*The Caledonian Mercury*—that he'd taken from the cottage this morning.

Opening it out he began to read, attempting to force from his mind all thoughts regarding his cousin, the broadsheet being a handy prop behind which to hide. He tried to focus on the columns of news, but his mind kept wandering back to Felicity and the prospect of her becoming Lady Gunn.

It wasn't the worst idea; she *was* of good breeding, she was a distant cousin and therefore not too close a family member for him to feel strange about the match, yet close enough that he felt a certain duty of care towards her and her situation. Polly would certainly benefit from a mother figure, and his daughter did appear to like the company of Ms. Adams. It might be something to consider over the course of the summer, should she still be available, of course.

Now, he wasn't sure if he wished her rendezvous in the

city to be successful or not. He had a sudden flashback to
Meriton House; its quiet, familiar warmth, and the
comforting privacy he found within its walls. No, he was not
ready for marriage, yet. Polly had Mrs. P., Miss Carmichael
and Miss Carter, and he certainly didn't need any more
females in his life at the moment.

That's it then, it is settled. A headline in the newspaper
caught his eye.

Missing City Lawyer Victim of Animal Attack

*Evelyn Robert Rosemont, partner at Rosemont & Gavill
Solicitors, has been confirmed as the second victim of a vicious
animal attack on the evening of May 16th.*

*Rosemont, formerly of Leith Street, Edinburgh, was
reported missing by his partner, Mr. Henry Gavill, two days
prior to the grisly discovery of Rosemont's body in an alleyway
near Princes Street.*

Rosemont & Gavill? That was the solicitors' firm he'd
visited the morning after he'd witnessed the attack in the
alley. So that was what the legal secretary had referred to as
'indisposed indefinitely'?

He glanced at the portfolio of real estate perched incon-
spicuously on the seat. That was the only evidence that
pointed towards any kind of connection to himself and the
dead lawyer. His skin prickled. Was it just a strange coincidence that one of the partners of the firm that had provided
him with that portfolio was now dead? He remembered the
empty mind of the victim, and the fact that he'd not been
able to glean any trace of memory from the dead man's
mind; almost as if it had been wiped clean... like the beast
had known of his ability to play voyeur to the dead. But that
was impossible. Whatever that beast was—rabid dog or

Barghest, according to Bobby Mac—it was an animal and certainly incapable of planning the murder of a lawyer he'd only ever communicated with via letter. It *had* to be an unfortunate coincidence, because the alternative was incomprehensible.

A shudder passed through him as he had a macabre thought: what if the beast wasn't exactly animal. He thought back to the day by the burn when he'd sensed the creature had been about to attack Polly. He'd thought then that there was something more to the beast but hadn't been able to put his finger on it.

What if the creature was somehow bound to Hemlock Nightingale? Midnight had been looking over his shoulder ever since those blasted goggles had been left on his doorstep. He didn't need to close his eyes to conjure the vision of Hemlock—possessed by a demonic force, ragged teeth, and rasping breath, hanging from the scaffolding of Westminster Bridge—and Polly's life hanging in the balance. *That* particular image had been permanently ingrained in his brain. It wasn't beyond the realms of possibility that his enemy had added some rabid creature to his ranks. Was it possible that Hemlock's reach spread this far from London? And if so, why wait eighteen months to make an appearance?

He let slip a huff of derision. *Paranoia is not a beneficial bedfellow. Get a hold of yourself, man.*

"Goodness. Are you all right, cousin? You've gone quite pale."

Midnight started at the sudden interruption of his thoughts and rallied himself quickly. He hadn't realised he'd lowered the newspaper, leaving his expression exposed to his companion. "Yes, thank you. I am fine. Just some troubling news in the Caledonian, nothing to worry about."

"Well, you certainly look worried." She glanced at the broadsheet on his lap, reading the headline. "Did you know him?"

"Not in person. But he worked for the firm that provided my portfolio."

"Oh! How unfortunate. The poor fellow. An animal attack? You don't think it's Bobby Mac's beastie surely?" she asked. Her skepticism showing in the narrowing of her eyes and the tilt of her head. "Didn't you mention something about a rabid dog?" The latter option clearly causing her the most concern.

"Something like that, yes," Midnight replied, not particularly wanting to engage in a conversation about the supernatural with her in front of Polly, who's attention had been snatched away from the scenery at the mention of the 'beastie'. As an afterthought he added, "Take care in the city this evening. I would not recommend any solo ventures through the streets after dark."

"Thank you for your concern, cousin. I will not be out *alone*."

Midnight noticed the inflection and the slight flush that rose in her cheeks. Yes, she was definitely meeting a suitor. He supposed his concern might seem like an overreaction, but he just could not shake the feeling that the attack on the lawyer and the episode in the woods with Polly was directed at him. Perhaps a trip into the city to talk with Inspector Anderson was in order, just to see if he could glean any further information about the case.

It was not long before the carriage stopped, leaving Midnight and Polly free to go on their way to Hooley House. Ms. Adams bid them farewell and Bobby Mac assured them he'd be back to collect them within the hour. Charlie, in all his wisdom, had decided to stay behind at the cottage. 'In case Miss Carter needs my help', he'd said, leaving Midnight with a lingering sense of guilt for making her cry in the first place.

The incident was still on his mind as they approached Hooley's extensive wrought iron gate, which was shut. Midnight shoved at it a little too roughly, and it swung open with a loud *creak*. He led Polly into the grounds which appeared to be well tended; the lawns were trimmed and the shrubbery beautifully carved into fanciful shapes that made Polly 'ohh' and 'ahh'. Midnight opened the portfolio to skim over the property details in which he noted that the house had only recently been put on the market and the family had not long moved out. That would account for the well-maintained gardens.

Polly practically ran up the steps to the very grand front entrance. Midnight could tell she was eager to explore. There was something of a shade of voyeurism about inspecting houses with a view to buying, running a critical eye over where people had placed furniture, their choice of décor—in this case, a little too ostentatious for Midnight's tastes—was unavoidable. Polly's enthusiasm declined visibly throughout the tour, as did his own.

"It's not right, is it, Miss Peeps?"

"Nah. It's too big and fancy. It's not *us*, Papa."

"You're absolutely right, sweetheart. It's not *us*." he smiled, always pleasantly surprised at how perceptive the girl was.

"'Sides, I can't fink Miss Carter'd be too happy about all the cleaning. Meriton's big enough, but this place is like Buckin'am bleedin' Palace!" She remembered her manners too late but had the good grace to look abashed at her choice of language.

Midnight struggled to suppress a smile; her crudeness

was quite endearing at times. Besides, she was right. It was like Buckingham bleeding Palace. "Right then, little miss. Onto the next one. We should have time to visit Caudwell Manor, providing Bobby Mac is back to pick us up."

"How far is that one?"

"It's just east of here, so perhaps another hour's ride. Do you think you can manage that?"

"I suppose so. Is it as big as this one?" She screwed up her top lip, unable to disguise her lack of enthusiasm.

"I don't think so," he chuckled. "It only has twelve bedrooms." He then laughed loudly as her face fell. "Poor Miss Peeps. I gather you thought house hunting would be somewhat more fun than this?"

"How many more will we be looking at this summer?" she asked, no doubt envisioning weeks of endless corridors, ballrooms, and bedrooms—enough to house a regiment.

"That depends on if we find a house that suits. I must say, the solicitor doesn't seem to have stuck to the brief I sent prior to my visit; I was hoping for something a little more rustic. If we're lucky, Caudwell might be the one and then we won't have to suffer any more."

"I 'ope so. I mean it's nice an' all, taking trips with you. But cor' blimey, me feet are plain worn out."

"Well then," he said, leading Polly back to the front door, "fingers crossed for Caudwell."

They made their way down the front steps to where the carriage was just visible coming up the long, tree-lined driveway. Polly waved vigorously and Bobby Mac raised a hand in reply. A few minutes later they were on their way again, Midnight having first ensured that his cousin had made it safely into the city.

"Aye, sir. I'm to pick the mistress up first thing in the morning from The George," the driver had said. The

George, Midnight had ascertained from Bobby Mac, was quite a luxurious establishment, and he'd wondered how Felicity could afford to stay there, even just for one night, considering her current financial situation.

About twenty minutes into the journey Midnight felt a sudden and powerful draw somewhere to his left. He looked out of the window but could see nothing but trees and the Pentland foothills. Still, the pull was so potent that he banged on the carriage roof and called for Bobby Mac to stop.

"What is it, Papa?" Polly asked.

"I don't know," Midnight replied. "Let's find out."

He exited the carriage and stepped off the road into the purple heather, searching. Polly jumped down after him, coming to join him at the roadside. He felt no danger just an irresistible sense of something calling to him. Spotting a very overgrown track through the brush, he turned to Bobby Mac. "What's down there?"

The driver's brows furrowed in deep thought as he tried to recall what might be at the end of that disused trail. "I'm no' rightly sure to be honest, sir."

"Will the carriage make it down the track?" Midnight waited while Bobby Mac made his assessment.

"I think so. We can give it a try, I suppose. If you really want te, I mean?" The driver looked a little dubious at the prospect. Midnight was hopeful the carriage would travel down the barely visible road, he could understand why the driver may not want to. It didn't look very welcoming at all. The thick tunnel-like overhang of tree branches and scrub disappeared into the distance, not allowing anyone a glimpse of what lay beyond.

"I think we must. There is something at the end of this

road that I need to see." There was a such a tone of certainty to his declaration he even surprised himself.

Bobby Mac dutifully turned the horses, and Midnight and Polly climbed back into the carriage. The journey suddenly became extremely uncomfortable as they were rocked and jolted from pillar to post by the seemingly endless bumpy track. Midnight almost began to rethink his decision to venture down it. But he could not deny the pull that compelled him towards whatever lay beyond the darkening tunnel of trees.

He checked his pocket watch. They'd been travelling down this new track for nearly half an hour and, as yet, had not reached the end. He was about to bang on the roof again when the carriage lurched to a halt, nearly throwing him from his seat.

"We're here, sir," Bobby Mac shouted and jumped down to open the door for his passengers.

The moment Midnight set foot upon the ground, he felt it. A pulse. There was a force so strong he could feel it in the air around him and in the ground at his feet. A sharp gasp behind him caused him to turn.

Polly stood agog, eyes wide with wonder. So she could feel it too?

He made his way awkwardly over the uneven ground to the front, where the horses were stamping their hooves and making small whinnies, snorting air from their nostrils in apparent agitation or impatience, he couldn't tell which.

Bobby Mac grabbed the lead horse's bridle and whispered calming words to it in Gaelic. The driver looked ahead, apprehension showing clearly on his weathered face. Midnight followed his gaze and his eyes fell upon a pair of tall, but badly rusted iron gates. One clung perilously on to the only hinge that prevented it from clattering to the ground. The walls that supported the gates were overgrown with ivy and crumbling in places. Whatever building these gates were protecting would likely be in the same state of dilapidation, but Midnight was more than curious to know the source of the intense energy that emanated from beyond those decaying walls. As he approached the gates he knew that he could force entry with one push of his power but Bobby Mac's presence prevented that. There was no possible way that the carriage would make it through them as they were.

"Bobby Mac, would you stay with the horses and Miss Polly, please? I'm going to take a look inside."

The Scot nodded but a wail of protest came from his daughter.

"Awww! But I wanna see too. Please, Papa?" She gave him such a pleading look that he nearly gave in.

"No, sweetheart. Not this time. We don't know what is beyond these gates." He squatted down next to her and lowered his voice. "I know you feel it, don't you?" Polly nodded and Midnight continued. "It could be dangerous. Let me go alone. I won't be too long, and I promise I'll tell you all about it when I return."

"Fine," she said, resigned and just a little grumpy, not at all happy about being left out of the adventure.

"I've some apples, miss. You can help me feed Starlight and Gorgon, if you like, aye?" Bobby Mac offered. The invitation went some way to placating the young miss, and she cheerily took Bobby's hand and let him lead her to the driver's seat where he kept the sack of apples.

Midnight nodded his thanks and squeezed himself through the skewed opening, moving as rapidly forward as the ground would allow. A growing sense of anticipation propelled him faster and faster through ever-thickening scrub. The sky was barely visible now through the canopy of tree branches that encapsulated him, but he was not afraid. He sensed no threat yet, just a rising thrum of mystical energy, pulsating and awake. When he finally broke through the mass of brush and branches, what he found took his breath away.

He stood facing the near ruins of a modest-sized castle. It waited there, hidden and protected by the forest that had become part of the building itself. Ivy and other indiscriminate climbing shrubbery adorned the facia from ground to roof. The odd tree branch could be seen protruding from the glassless windows. The old wooden door swung freely to and fro in the breeze, the metallic creak of rusty hinges strangely in tune with the sigh of the wind through the forest. He noted the words carved into the stone lintel above—*Cnoc Sithe*. The ancient stone called to him.

And he answered. As he stepped cautiously through the humble entrance—for this was not a grand building by today's standards—he felt the welcoming touch of home.

"Cor!" came the awed whisper of a voice he knew all too well. He didn't need to turn to know Polly and Bobby Mac were behind him; he could sense their wonderment. He should have known the little minx would find some way of wheedling her way to him. She was far too curious for her own good but he echoed her sentiment.

"Sorry, sir. She was worried about you and was quite determined to come and find you with or without me." Bobby Mac shrugged apologetically.

Midnight gave his wayward daughter a look through lowered brows, but she didn't qualm. She was far too distracted by her surroundings, and he couldn't blame her; they were sublime. "It's fine, Bobby. I know how she can be."

He smiled, then said to Polly, "Well then, seeing as you're here, shall we take a look around?"

"Oh, yes!" she replied excitedly.

"Very well, *but* there are rules, young lady. If you do not follow those rules then it's back to the carriage with a spanked bottom for you," he threatened. Polly grinned, knowing full well that her father would never spank her, he rarely even scolded her and so the threat caused her no concern. "You *must* stay with me—no wandering off—and don't touch *anything*. Do you understand?" he said in his sternest paternal voice.

"Yeah, 'course I do. I won't go nowhere wivout you. I promise." Midnight looked unconvinced. "I swear." Polly held aloft her stump with practiced innocence. She caught the twinkle in her father's eye and beamed.

"I shall hold you to that, Polly Peeps. And if you break your promise, then no pudding this evening." He winked, and she came over to stand by him and slipped her tiny good hand into his large one. "Ready?"

"Um-hmm"

"I'll away back to the horses if you please, sir?"

"Of course. We won't be long. Thank you, Bobby."

Bobby Mac left, relieved. It appeared something about the place had him on edge. It was better for Midnight if Bobby wasn't present just in case he had cause to use his powers.

Polly and Midnight meandered through the ruined rooms, hand in hand. His reverence for this sleeping stone giant was undeniable. The moss-covered walls, the carpet of dry leaves, and the odour of time enveloped him in their powerful embrace. Although the atmosphere was palpable, a distinct sense of peacefulness settled over him. He felt the watchful eyes of ancient turrets and ramparts wash over him, awakened from their dormant guardianship and alive with his new and long-awaited presence. 'You're home,' they said to him.

And he knew it.

So did Polly, she squeezed his hand gently and looked up at him, the beginnings of happy tears glistened at the corners of her big, brown eyes. "This is the one," she whispered.

"Yes," he agreed. "Yes, it is." He would need to go into the city, of course, to make enquiries as to the name and where-abouts of any owner. And he would stop by the lawyers' office to set things in motion but also to see if he could find out anything more about that animal attack and the unfortunate death of Mr. Rosemont.

For now, he invited Polly for a quick exploration of the exterior and grounds. He assumed there *were* grounds but that the forest had long since reclaimed any formal gardens. Midnight decided he liked the wild, rugged look, it added to the secluded privacy he so craved. They found their way to the rear of the castle. The back door was swollen shut, the oak still strong despite its age. It looked like it opened inwards so there was no point in trying to kick it open. Instead, he summoned his powers, mixing a little light with the shade this time, not wanting to taint the structure with purely dark energy. Tendrils of gold wove around the smoke that emanated from his hands. He was most formidable when his powers were mixed, something he'd only recently discovered. The light gave him balance and control over his darker side and lessened the pain of hosting the shadows. At the height of his power, he could move mountains— metaphorically speaking— and so the stubborn door gave him no trouble. It gave a meagre groan of protest then popped open, bathing them both in the glow of the afternoon sun.

"Ooo!" cried Polly.

Ooo indeed, thought Midnight. The view that presented itself was nothing short of spectacular. There was, he estimated, around fifty yards or more of flat, overgrown brush that gave way to a gently rising, tree-covered hill. And the top of that hill was where the mysterious energy originated. As soon as his gaze fell upon that rounded peak, he knew it. Peacefulness was replaced by sheer awe. He could see nothing through the trees, but he knew he *must* go there.

But not with Polly in tow. No, it was too dangerous. His senses could not determine whether the energy was benign or malignant. It was just pure power, and that scared him a little. If this castle was to be their summer home, he needed to know exactly what waited at the top of that hill.

7

MISUNDERSTANDINGS

Midnight waited all of the next day for the return of Felicity Adams from Edinburgh. By six that evening, he couldn't decide if he should be concerned or frustrated at her lack of appearance. He needed Bobby Mac to drive him to the city so he could make enquiries about the abandoned castle. He'd sent Charlie up to the main house and stables countless times in his impatience and was now plagued by a growing concern for his cousin's welfare. The only thing that quelled his concern was that Bobby had not returned either and so must've stayed in the city to wait for his mistress to conclude her business. Surely, if she was planning on staying another night, Bobby Mac would've returned by now?

"Dinner'll be ready soon, sir. I made plenty for everyone, since there's no word of an invitation from the big house this evening."

"Hmm?" Midnight turned from his window vigil to see that it was Miss Carter who had interrupted his thoughts. He immediately softened. "Right. Thank you. Yes. No invitation. It seems our gracious host is staying late in the city."

Miss Carter bobbed a curtsey and left. Midnight offered a last glance in the direction of the big house before joining the rest of them at the kitchen table. It was a simple meal of cock-a-leekie, the broth having been made from the leftovers of yesterday's roasted cockerel and served with freshly baked and buttered cobs. Miss Carter had done a splendid job with the old rooster and cooked him well enough that the meat wasn't too tough. Midnight admitted to feeling a little guilty about enjoying the taste of the 'lord of the yard' given his untimely demise. He complimented Miss Carter on the two hearty meals she'd managed to produce from the old feathered fiend. Her culinary skills were not a patch on Mrs. P.'s, but the meal was hot and hearty with plenty of flavor, and he was pleased to see his compliments so well received.

Miss Carter never looked so pretty as she did when her cheeks flushed that very alluring shade of pale pink. Midnight thought she would make someone a fine wife one day and shocked himself with the mental image of Miss Carter as a married woman. He was shocked because he found the idea entirely to his distaste.

Hastily dispelling the thought from his mind, he gulped down the rest of the dinner and made his excuses. It was almost sunset and he'd decided to take a quick stroll over to the big house to see if his cousin had returned and if she had not, he would ask Craigson if he'd had word from his mistress.

"No word as yet, sir." Craigson said.

"And Mr. MacDonald hasn't returned either?"

"No, sir."

"Hmm. It's a little concerning, don't you think? Your mistress was due home hours ago."

"I expect her meeting has run on longer than she anticipated is all," Craigson offered. Then, almost as an afterthought, he said, "Would sir like to wait in the drawing room for her return? I can fetch the sherry—"

"Brandy," Midnight interrupted. He couldn't stomach the sherry. "Thank you. I will wait for a short time, at least."

Craigson nodded and escorted Midnight to the drawing room, leaving him then to fetch the brandy. Midnight strolled directly over to the fireplace which, he was sorry to find, was not lit. He shivered. Clearly the household was not expecting guests this evening or the imminent return of its mistress. He walked determinedly towards the drawing room door and back out into the hallway calling loudly for the butler who promptly appeared, tray in hand.

"Sir?"

"Thank you, Craigson," Midnight replied as the man held forth the tray with the decanted alcohol and cut-glass crystal tumbler on it. He had been about to decline and leave but changed his mind, poured out a large measure and gulped it down in one go. The amber liquid burned as it slid down his throat and warmed his stomach, immediately quelling some of his worry. "I'll have my coat, if you please?"

"Is sir leaving already?" the butler asked in a disinterested tone.

"Yes. No point waiting. Have Mr. MacDonald send word to the cottage upon Ms. Adams' return."

"Certainly, sir."

Midnight didn't know why he felt suddenly irritated, but he did. "Leave the coat. I'll get it myself on the way out." He strode past Craigson, not even waiting for a reply, grabbed his coat from the hook and left.

The chill of the evening was warded off by the brandy that now began to percolate through his veins, his irritation dissipating along with the warm feeling in his blood. *What concern is it of yours how the lady chooses to spend her days, or nights for that matter?* He couldn't fathom why he was agitated at the mere fact that his cousin had not returned. Something unpleasant tickled the very depths of his subconscious, and he didn't like it. Since his arrival in Scotland, he couldn't shake the feeling that he had an invisible target on his back. As the minutes passed, his conviction grew, practically convincing him that Felicity's absence had something to do with him.

You utter arse, he thought to himself. "I couldn't agree more," he said aloud as he shucked on his coat and stomped down the path towards the cottage.

The cottage was quiet when he entered. A welcome glow emanated from the kitchen to the right and from the parlour to the left. He hung up his coat and stuck his head around the parlour door. It was empty. Good. He needed solitude. This fire was lit, and he took a seat next to it. Only two of the candle sconces were lit, bathing the little room in a cosy blanket of dim yellow—enough to keep the shadows at bay. They called to him more when he was in a bad mood. The calming effect of the brandy had worn off. He glanced around for the crystal decanter he knew to be in this room but couldn't see it on the sideboard. He was about to get up and venture into the kitchen for a discreet scouting mission when he heard a tentative knock on the parlour door.

"Yes?" he said a little too sharply. The door opened slowly. He saw the tray first, then the decanter of brandy and a glass, followed by Miss Carter sporting a shy but welcoming smile.

"Begging your pardon, sir, but I heard you come in and thought you might like a drink?"

"You must have read my mind." Midnight smiled back, his annoyance instantly receding. "I was just looking for that."

"Apologies. I'd taken it to the kitchen to warm by the fire. I know how you like it warm."

Midnight inadvertently looked at the fire in the parlour and then flicked his eyes towards Miss Carter whose cheeks bore her signature shade. She busied herself by placing the tray on the sideboard and pouring him a large glass. He came to stand beside her, eager for another taste of the excellent beverage. It was a good vintage. She put the stopper in the decanter and set it down in its usual place then reached for the glass at the same time he did. His fingers brushed the back of her hand, and she let out an involuntary gasp.

"Beg pardon—"

"Sorry—"

They both laughed nervously at their simultaneous apology. She was so pretty when she smiled. She was pretty when she wasn't smiling too. Midnight held her gaze for a second, long enough to notice the longing behind them. Emotions were rolling from her in waves—a whirlpool of desire, fear, anticipation, and something else... shame? His brow creased. Her gaze dropped, his own followed and came to rest upon his hand clasped around hers. His thumb traced a line of faint freckles that dappled the back of it. She shuddered. He became acutely aware of his own emotions. A pounding beat quickened in his chest as he realised how perilously close to each other they stood. His underarms prickled, his collar suddenly felt too tight, and he gulped loudly.

Let go of her hand, you cad! his inner conscience

screamed. But he could not let go. Her skin was velvet, addictive. The charged silence between them rang louder than a church bell. He lifted his gaze once more, nervous to see that longing in her eyes again. Her face was cast downwards. Miss Carter would not look at him. Midnight let go of her hand at last.

"Miss Polly is in bed an— and Miss Carmichael too." She gulped.

"Mm-hmm," he murmured. "And Charlie?"

"S— staying at the stables. Waiting for Bobby to come 'ome." Her voice was low, almost a whisper.

He concentrated on her mouth as she struggled to form words. Repressed power bubbled inside of him. He was teetering on the edge of something dark and unknown. "Just us then." His own voice was now a low and sultry whisper. What in God's name was happening here? Miss Carter's breathing came in rapid, shallow bursts. Her bosom rose and fell in a glorious swell of pale, freckled invitation. "Laura—" he growled.

"Please." Miss Carter stood before him, those beautifully pink-flushed cheeks now a burning red. Faint traces of tears had begun to form in her eyes.

Midnight stepped back. "I am sorry. I—" He started to apologise, appalled at his ungentlemanly, uncontrolled behaviour.

She shook her head vigorously. "Don't," she gasped "I didn't want—"

The front door swung open and in barrelled Charlie, shouting as he burst into the hallway. "Your lordship? Are you home? Come quickly. There's been an accident!"

Midnight's head shot towards the parlour room door and then back to Miss Carter who was rapidly scrubbing her hand across her face whilst trying to avoid looking at him. She straightened her apron and left the room without so much as a glance in his direction. Midnight was left with an unpleasant hollow feeling. Had he just crossed a line from which he would never be able to recover?

8

MISSING

"We've gathered men and formed a search party," Inspector Anderson said, his words coming out in uneven spurts as the police carriage bound along at speed over the uneven country road.

"Good. And the driver, any word from him?" Midnight's face was creased with concern. He'd been right to be worried about his cousin.

"Being fixed up at the Royal Infirmary last I knew. He was conscious when he was found, but the witness tells me he passed out directly after the rescue and never regained consciousness."

"Tell me again what he said."

Inspector Anderson got out his notebook and held it up to the window attempting to read his notes but the light was rapidly fading from the blue twilight to the orange death throes of the spring sunset. "Ach! I canna see." Anderson declared, his Scottish accent slipping through. "I remember he said that the driver—"

"Bobby MacDonald."

"Aye. I remember he said something about the driver muttering about a ghost or a beastie of some sort. Something drove them off the road. I'm thinking the driver was probably pished and is making excuses for his mistake. I certainly don't believe in ghosts and there's no single 'beastie' in this country big enough to overturn a carriage, that's for sure."

"What about these rabid dogs you say may be roaming around, the ones responsible for the two killings? Could it be one of those?"

"Possible but highly unlikely, aye? I mean even a bloody great dog would get crushed under the carriage wheels, it wouldnae be big enough to cause that amount of carnage on its own. It could have been a pack of the buggers, I suppose."

"Hmm. And the witness didn't see anything?"

"No. He only discovered the wreckage because his own horse threw him off and bolted. By the time he'd found the bugger, he'd wandered off the main road and down the hillside, which is where he found them, carriage all broken to bits, and the driver pinned underneath it. No sign of Ms. Adams or the horses."

Midnight wondered what had happened to the animals. He hoped his cousin had managed to mount one and either make her way home or to some close-by sanctuary where she might be awaiting rescue. His sympathies were with Bobby Mac also. He was a decent fellow and he'd been severely injured.

Midnight would ensure he would be cared for properly until his recovery. The voluntary hospitals weren't renowned for their stellar treatment of the layman, although he had Anderson's reassurance that Bobby would be looked after well enough. Nevertheless, he would arrange for Bobby's transfer back to Glenhaven as soon as he was fit enough, and he'd pay for a private physician to attend him.

The situation put him in mind of his own charity hospital in London; the building by the docks had been undergoing its transformation from abandoned warehouse to hospital for the poor for the best part of fifteen months. There was still a long way to go before it was ready for patients but it was coming along nicely. Giles had helped him source a project management team and they had already shortlisted a number of surgeons and nurses, the latter being recruited from Miss Florence Nightingale's college of nurses. He'd been honoured to meet Miss Nightingale last summer and had found her to be a singular, insightful sort of person showing aptitude and forethought. Her theories on hospital hygiene and sanitation were fascinating, and he was keen to implement the same ideas at his own, Saint Francis' Charitable Hospital.

Their carriage slowed to a halt, and Midnight could see a number of people from his window, silhouetted against the glare of flaming torches, gathered together and listening to a man shouting instructions. Inspector Anderson exited first, holding the door open for Midnight.

"This way, your Lordship." Anderson turned and made his way towards the party of men.

A burly fellow with a shaggy beard was handing out lighted torches, and the policeman next to him was sorting people into three groups. The policeman glanced up at their approach.

"Constable Mooney." Anderson greeted him.

"Sir."

"This is Lord Gunn. He's Ms. Adams's cousin and will be helping with the search."

Mooney nodded at Midnight who nodded back. "You'll

be needing a light then. Danny, gi' his Lordship a torch aye?"
The burly bearded 'Danny' handed Midnight a burning
branch. "You can join yonder group. They'll be walkin' the
road. Shouldnae be too dirty aye." Mooney instructed,
looking him up and down, noting his tailored attire.

Midnight was grateful for the relative darkness to hide
his irked expression but then wondered if 'walking the road'
might be the best thing. It would allow him access to both
the lower part of the hill and the upper, should the need
arise. It was easy enough to drop back from the group and
slip away. He had no intention of staying with them. His
talents were needed tonight, and he did not want an
audience.

His designated group set off up the road at a slow pace.
Ms. Adams's name was being shouted at random intervals
while men swiped at the roadside brush with sticks, looking
for any sign of the missing woman. Midnight shut out the
noise of the men's shouts and focused his mind on his
cousin, searching for her energy among the tall, shadowy
forms of the trees on either side of the road. An owl hooted
somewhere nearby and then abruptly cut short and was
silent. It was this that pricked his attention.

He stood still and listened, letting the others forge
ahead. Nobody noticed him slip silently away into the
forest's dark embrace. The trees acted like a buffer, muffling
the sounds of the search party and replacing the shouts and
the swoop of sticks with the undulating swishing of the
night breeze through branch and leaf. Treading carefully,
Midnight made his way down the hillside, the glow from his
torch lighting his way just enough to prevent him from
turning an ankle on the rugged ground. Pine needles and
dry twigs crunched under his feet, loud in the eerily silent
wood. The shadows tugged at his skin, urgent and eager,

and all sounds faded into nothing. The trees grew still and the breeze settled somewhat. It was as if the whole of the forest held its breath and watched.

Midnight opened himself to the darkness, and the shadows poured into him. He greeted them in painful welcome, careful to balance the darkness within with a thin sliver of the light from the flaming torch he held. The light kept him in control, the lion tamer to the lion. Immediately, his senses became heightened. He scanned his surroundings and sensed the energies of the woodland animals that lay quivering in their burrows or clinging tightly and unmoving to the branches above. They were afraid. That much he knew. But of what? Himself, or something else? Pushing further with his mind, he picked up on the faintest life force somewhere in the thick undergrowth ahead.

The torch in his left hand, lighting the way, Midnight curled the fingers of his right hand allowing a swirling pool of black smoke to emanate from his palm. He held it there, ready to shoot at any foe who may attempt to spring a surprise attack. As he advanced, he noticed the trees thinning out a little until he could see a small clearing ahead. The moonlight shone just enough for him to make out a large shape on the ground. The pool of smoke roiled as he prepared to launch it, but he hesitated, not sensing any direct threat. The shape quivered and issued a soft snort. It tried to raise its head but failed.

Midnight, realising he was in no danger, let the smoke ball dissipate and hurried forward to aid what was clearly an injured animal. He spoke in gentle shushing tones as he knelt beside the poor creature. Jamming the torch into the ground, he reached for the sleek equine head of his cousin's carriage horse, Starlight.

"There now, Starlight. Hush," he soothed, laying his

hand on the grey's forelock. "It's all right, girl. It's all right. What happened to you? And where is your mistress, hmm?" He kept his voice low and monotone to calm the distressed beast. Running his hand over the mare's ears and down her neck, he was not shocked to find his hand came away stained with blood; he'd smelled the unmistakable coppery tang on the faint breeze.

Drawing power from the torchlight, he channeled a thin sliver of healing power through his hands into the shuddering flesh of the horse. Starlight whinnied in response, sensing her saviour's purpose. The flow of blood stemmed enough for him to perform a hasty examination. The horse had several large gashes to her throat and shoulders consistent with the claw marks of a large predator.

"Poor girl. I'll fix you right up. Just lay still." Midnight knew he could heal her. He'd found her just in time. A few more bursts of his healing energy would do the trick. He had an idea. "Let me have a little look in your head while I'm at it, eh?" Penetrating the memories of an animal was as easy to perform as it was on a human, the difficulty came in interpreting the images. Not to mention the fact that he'd only ever performed this trick on lifeless corpses. Nevertheless, he knew he must try. He must know if this was the act of Bobby Mac's devilish 'Barghest'.

Tiny pinpricks of pain crossed his palm as he withdrew the light from the injured mare and replaced it with the shadows. Easing his power into the mind of the inert Starlight, he began to search for the horses most recent memories in his own mind. It worked; he heard the clip-clopping of two sets of hooves on the road, the soft whinnies of communication between Starlight and Gorgon. Seeing events through the eyes of an animal felt entirely alien to

Midnight but he forced himself to focus, to be alert and watchful for any clues.

He couldn't be sure but it felt like both the carriage horses had been nervous; the reproachful shouts of Bobby Mac echoed in his mind. A whip cracked, and Gorgon tossed his head in protest, ears pressed tightly back in alarm. Starlight snorted in answer then missed a step as something large and shaggy raced across the path in front of her. There was a scream—a woman's scream. Ms. Adams? It had to be—then a jumble of images and blood-curdling growls. The two horses, now finding their reins freed, took flight, and the carriage bounced along at frightening speed. The shaggy black shape raced alongside barking and howling. Starlight, her heart pounding with fear, veered towards it in an effort to run it off the road. It disappeared under the carriage. More growling penetrated the thunderous noise of wheels and whinnies. The carriage jerked, and Gorgon's harness snapped, releasing him to run on ahead. Starlight flattened her head and raced after her companion, but the weight of the carriage held her back. Now off-kilter, the carriage bounced and rocked erratically. Something landed on her back, and she squealed in pain. Claws tore at her throat causing her to kick and buck. Her own harness came free, and she fled, leaving the carriage to tumble away behind her. She managed to throw off her attacker and run downhill into the safety of the forest. Blood poured from her wounds, and she had no choice but to slow, eventually succumbing to weariness.

Midnight released himself from the horse's mind. "It's been quite the night for you, hasn't it, girl?" he said quietly as he laid his hands on the half-healed wounds and channeled more light into the scarred flesh. "There now. That's better, isn't it?" He patted her gently and rose. "Up you get, Starlight. Good girl."

The horse snorted and lifted her head as if testing herself. Upon realising she could move, she got steadily to her feet and shook out her bloodied mane. She stood still for a moment, swishing her tail and eyeing Midnight with a cautious air. He held out his hand for her to sniff. She took a step forward and nuzzled his open palm.

"Are we friends now?" he asked the mare.

She snickered lightly in response, flicked her head once and took off into the night.

"Hey!" he shouted after her fleeing form. "You are *most* welcome!" he finished wryly. "I suppose I can cross Horse-Whisperer off my list of talents."

Grabbing his torch, which had begun to sputter, he took in his surroundings. Should he continue on into the forest or make his way back to the road? A sudden cracking of twigs caused the hair on the back of his neck to rise. Focusing his mind, he sensed an energy behind him, wary and watchful.

Smoke balled in his hand once more, ready to strike. Using his enhanced senses, he probed further, investigating the energy. *Animal...* he surmised. *Dangerous?* Midnight shifted his stance in an effort to see what watched him from the security of the tree line and was rewarded with a low, warning growl.

"Hello, beastie," he murmured. And turned his head to face his foe head on.

At first, he saw nothing, but as he stared intently at the spot from where he estimated the growl had come, his eyes made out the shadowy form of a large four-legged creature.

"Let me get a proper look at you then, *Master of Shadows*," Midnight cooed, standing his ground.

The creature responded with a slow, purposeful step forward. The moonlight bathed the beast in an ethereal glow as it emerged into the clearing, unfazed and oozing with deadly confidence. Two piercing eyes, large and oblique, pinned him with an appraising glare. The head, lupine in appearance, hung low, its gaping maw displaying alarmingly long canines. Jaw like a shovel, the animal pushed forward into full view, brazen and cocksure. The forepaws, as large as a lion's, made little noise on the forest floor as it strode toward the human who challenged it.

Midnight raised his arm, displaying the roiling ball of dark power in his hand, and the wolf-like beast snarled in warning, eyes flashing. Midnight stood his ground, prepared to attack, but the animal made no move to spring. It seemed more intent on displaying its great mass and power.

They stood for a moment, face to face, like boxers in a ring, each one assessing the other, noting strengths and possible weaknesses. The thing was huge, even for a wolf. Although Midnight wasn't even sure it was a wolf; at first glance it could easily pass for one, but upon closer inspection, its body was much larger and different in proportion to any such wolf or dog he'd ever seen. It reminded him of something he'd read recently in an American scientific journal. The article had described a dire wolf. Midnight wondered if Anderson's rabid dog was in fact a captured dire wolf, perhaps bound for a zoo, that had escaped from a ship docked in Leith. It was a possibility, but this specimen looked different to the illustration he remembered. It was covered in shaggy fur which was thicker around its withers and neck, not unlike a lion's mane. The ears were elongated and triangular with exaggerated tufted tips and the tail was shorter and thicker than he would've expected, club-like even. The beast flicked the appendage menacingly almost as if it had understood Midnight's evaluation.

Midnight cocked his head in acknowledgement. "Fancy your chances, do you?"

The thing licked its lips greedily, its tongue languishing a second too long on one of its menacing canines.

Midnight's heart skipped a beat in a brief moment of self-doubt. Fighting Hemlock Nightingale in his hideous, creature form had proved testing. Would he be a match for this gigantic relic from a bygone age?

"What *are* you?" he demanded.

The moon slipped behind a cloud shrouding the clearing in sudden inky blackness. The creature threw back its head and howled long and loud, forcing Midnight to relinquish his dark power and clap both hands over his ears for fear the unholy sound might burst his eardrums. The howl died off when the moon reappeared; the creature had gone.

"Well, Bobby Mac. I think I just found your Barghest."

9

BODYSNATCHED

Breakfast was a tense affair. Miss Carmichael stood at the kitchen stove in place of Miss Carter, who had not emerged from her bedroom at all this morning, salting the porridge and serving three very sullen people.

"Can I go upstairs and visit with Laura after breakfast, Papa?" Polly mumbled through her porridge-filled mouth.

Midnight coughed. "Not today young lady. Miss Carter is apparently sick and must rest." He stirred his tea vigorously, the spoon rattling loudly against the china cup. "And don't speak with your mouth full."

Swallowing, Polly replied, "Sorry."

Charlie had been at the stables all night with Starlight who had been found making her way home to Glenhaven tired and in some distress. He was now tapping his feet impatiently on the stone floor of the kitchen, eager to get back to tend her. With Bobby Mac in hospital and Midnight's cousin still missing, Midnight had taken it upon himself to appoint Charlie as temporary stable master and Charlie was taking his new role very seriously.

"How is the horse?" Midnight enquired.

"Right shaken up she is, poor mare. I should be getting back soon." Charlie said with a purposeful glance at Agnes. She obliged by pushing a bowl of the hot oatmeal towards him. He began shoveling his cereal into his mouth at speed. "Them wounds round her neck is 'ealing a treat, mind." He sputtered and Polly frowned at her father waiting for him to reproach Charlie for speaking with a mouth full of food as he had her.

She was most put out when he didn't. Slamming her spoon down on the table and folding her arms, she fixed Midnight with an indignant scowl.

"Miss Polly!" Agnes hissed through her teeth.

"Well 'ow come Charlie don't get a rollicking, eh?" Polly demanded.

"Hush, child. Mind your manners." Midnight cut in.

"Seems to me it's everyone else whose manners need mindin'. Poor Laura's in her sick bed and ain't nobody finking she might be sad. Instead, everyone's got a face like a—"

"I said *hush!*" Midnight banged his hand on the table, making them all jump.

Silence struck the room. Charlie halted his spoon midway to his mouth and promptly closed it with an audible *pop!* Polly stood up abruptly, her chair scraping on the stone floor. Tears brimmed in her eyes then trickled down her cheeks in fat rivulets.

"Polly, I'm sorry." Midnight, immediately regretting his harsh words, reached for the child but she wrenched her arm away.

"No, you ain't! You're upset about Ms. Adams, and so are we, but it don't mean you can behave like a grumpy old badger. I *will* go visit wiv Laura, and you can't stop me!"

Polly, fist clenched, turned on her heels and stomped out of the room, slamming the kitchen door behind her.

Agnes and Charlie both looked like they'd like a dark corner to hide in at this very moment. Midnight sat, thin-lipped and eyes closed, breathing deeply and slowly trying to contain his temper. He could not afford to lose control in front of the governess. Charlie perceptively changed tack and asked Agnes to help him fetch fresh water and oats for Starlight. She didn't waste any time in agreeing, and the pair of them skedaddled out of the room faster than rabbits down a hole.

Grateful for the silence, Midnight kept his eyes closed for a few more minutes. He massaged his temples and relaxed, letting in the morning light to calm his nerves. Polly, ridiculously observant for her age, had been right, of course. His concern for the safety and whereabouts of his cousin grew by the hour. The previous night's search having turned up nothing but an injured horse, Inspector Anderson had called an end to it just after two o'clock in the morning.

He'd assured Midnight they would resume the search come first light, but as yet, no messenger or carriage had come to the cottage. He checked his pocket watch: twenty after seven. He supposed it was still quite early. Perhaps the inspector and his men were still getting organised. He would wait another hour and then see if Starlight was fit enough to ride.

"What to do?" he asked himself, fingers drumming on the table top. Heaving himself up with a sigh, he took a last sip of tea, wiped his mouth on a napkin, and prepared to go head to head with the most stubborn creature he had ever come across.

Midnight could hear the soft sniffles coming from Polly's

room before he reached the top of the stairs, and his stomach felt as though a huge stone weighed heavy inside it. He regretted shouting at her and felt immensely guilty for having made her cry. Patience was not one of his virtues and the little of it he had was tested daily by the vivacious wee Devil. Still, he should know better. He was the adult and therefore should be in control of his emotions and actions when it came to parenting. If truth be known, it was the guilt and shame he felt over the incident with Miss Carter, and her subsequent self-extraction from the breakfast party this morning that had added to the tensions he already held over his cousin's disappearance. He would not have normally lost his temper so easily with Polly but for that.

Miss Carter's room was opposite Polly's, and he hesitated a moment outside the door, listening for any signs of life. He raised a knuckle, debating whether or not to knock to see if she was all right but stepped away at the last second.

Bloody coward. Turning instead to the other door, he knocked gently. "Polly, sweetheart. May I come in?"

He heard a loud snort, like she was blowing her nose and then a defiant "S'pose so. Can't stop ya."

Midnight turned the handle and pushed the door gently open. Poking his head around it, he saw Polly. She stood with her back to him and her arms folded tightly across her chest, head held high. He opened the door fully and stepped into his daughter's cosy little room.

"May I sit?" A one shouldered shrug was all the answer he received. "I am sorry for shouting. I didn't mean to upset you. You were right about Ms. Adams. I am very worried about her, but I should not have taken it out on you. Am I forgiven?"

The little girl turned to face him. She wiped her hand under her nose then scrubbed the hand on her skirts.

Midnight did his best not to cringe—he did not do well with phlegm. Blood and guts he could handle, but phlegm was an entirely different matter. The little girl considered him, her head cocked to one side. "Your colours are darker," she said matter-of-factly.

"They are?" Midnight tried to think of the last time his daughter had mentioned seeing his colours or anyone else's, for that matter. It had been a long time. He glanced at her neck to see if he could spot the chain that held the special labradorite pendant she always wore tucked under her clothes.

Polly shook her head. "Not your face, your *colours.* They're all... mucky."

Midnight self-consciously ran a hand over his face as if to check that the terrifying half-human half-skull façade that Polly had one seen wasn't showing.

Polly's one remaining hand went to the chain around her neck, and she plucked at it with her delicate fingers. Raising the stumped arm, she waved it at him and said. "Yeah, all round the top of your 'ead. Looks dirty," she finished and wrinkled her nose.

Midnight, unsure of an appropriate response to this information merely uttered a surprised noise.

Polly, knowing she now had the floor, continued. "It ain't Ms. Adams what's got your colours muddied. It's Laura."

"What?" Midnight spluttered, taken aback at the unabashed perceptiveness of his daughter.

"Mmhm. They always turn funny when you're near Laura lately. Have you had a fallin' out or somfink? Is she really sick?"

"I—" His hand went to his forehead. He was suddenly sweating. "We... No, we didn't have an— That is to say..." He stopped talking and drew in a deep breath before continuing. "We did not have an argument. *Miss Carter*—" He deliberately emphasised the housemaid's proper title of address. "—is ill. And she needs to rest. That is all. As for my colours being 'muddy': I have rather a lot on my mind. It stands to reason they might be a little off." He hadn't meant to sound so defensive and was aware that his tone had come across as a tad harsh. He sighed, suddenly weary. He'd meant to come in here and soothe the waters between himself and Polly, and yet the little minx had somehow managed to turn the tables on him and make *him* feel like the one whose behaviour was up for debate. A victorious smirk spread across Polly's cherubic face and he found he couldn't help but smile back at her.

"Am I forgiven?" he asked, resignedly.

"Depends." was her answer.

"On?"

"Whether or not you say sorry to Laura."

"But—" he began in protest and then stopped. He *did* need to apologise to Miss Carter but not for the reasons Polly thought. "Fine. I'll apologise as soon as I'm able." Assuming, he thought, that Miss Carter ever ventured outside of her room ever again. A shameful flush graced his cheeks again. *Dammit!* He really needed to get past the embarrassment of what had occurred between him and his housemaid. The sooner he faced her and admitted his wrong doing, the sooner they could get back to some semblance of normality in his household.

Polly was in his arms in a flash, hugging him tightly. "I'm sorry too, Papa." Her voice muffled against his collar.

"What for?"

"For being an unruly imp and shouting back at you during breakfast." she sniffed and Midnight couldn't help but chuckle.

"Well now, if that isn't an understatement, I don't know what is." He smiled and tugged one of her curls. "Unruly and impish you may be at times, dearest girl, but you're also the kindest, most perceptive, and self-assured young lady I have ever had the misfortune to meet." He tickled her, and she giggled, squirming in his arms. Her raucous laughter was infectious, and he was soon laughing with her. Their frivolity was very suddenly interrupted by the loud bang of the front door and Charlie's shouting.

"Sir? 'Ere, look! Sir?"

The summons continued in animated exuberance as Midnight made his way downstairs to investigate the commotion. He found Charlie in the front hallway madly waving the morning newspaper around and hopping frantically from one foot to another.

The stableman thrust the paper into his employers hands. "It's front page news, sir, look!" Midnight shook out the crumpled paper and read the headline.

"Bodysnatched?" he exclaimed, reading quickly on.

"What else does it say?" Charlie demanded. He could read well enough to make out the main headline and the lessons he'd had from Agnes the last few months enabled him to read a few other simple phrases, but he was keen to know all the gory details. After all, it was not every day a corpse disappeared from a morgue.

Midnight read aloud, "The body of Evelyn Rosemont, city lawyer, has been stolen from Edinburgh morgue. Rosemont, tragically killed on May 16th, was under the care of the Gary Street morgue. However, on the morning of the 18th, the mortician made his way down to the underground basement whereupon he made the grisly discovery. Relatives have been informed and the police investigation is ongoing."

"Who would want to steal his body?" Miss Carmichael, who had come from the kitchen, cut in. "And why?"

"Who indeed?" Midnight was intrigued. As he skimmed the report, he found mention of more bodies mysteriously going missing. "As for why, perhaps Edinburgh has another Burke and Hare on its hands." Shocked gasps followed this statement, both Agnes and Charlie had heard of the notorious murderers and body snatchers who had plagued the city more than thirty years ago.

"Surely not?" Agnes asked in disbelief.

"I suppose it's a possibility." Midnight concluded. Although, he wasn't yet convinced. Could it be mere coincidence that the body of his own lawyer had been taken on the very same day of his cousin's accident and subsequent disappearance?

"Somefink stinks," declared Charlie.

"Indeed it does."

"Nah, I mean *really* whiffs. Phoah! What is that pong?"

All three of them sniffed the air before Agnes suddenly cried out, "The porridge pot! I left it on the stove." And off she rushed in a blur of swishing skirts.

"Blimey, I hope Miss Carter ain't sick for too long. Miss Carmichael ain't much of a cook." Charlie nodded toward the doorway that Agnes had just rushed through. "Though she does try." He amended, thinking his previous words might sound unkind.

"Hopefully not too long. I shall enquire after Miss Carter presently." Midnight resigned himself to the fact that he would have to face the girl sooner or later, and it might as well be sooner. "Is Starlight fit for riding yet?"

"Not really, sir. She's awful twitchy and them scars still ain't fully 'ealed. 'Appen another day or two and she'll be right."

"I see. What about one of the other horses in the stables?"

"There's Ms. Adams horse, I suppose, but she might be a tad small for you. The only other one is Samson. I swear he's the devil's spawn. He tried taking a nag out of me this morning when I gave him his oats."

"Meet me at the stables in half an hour? I need to ride into the city."

"Yes sir." Charlie doffed his cap and left the cottage. Midnight entered the kitchen to find a flustered governess wrestling with a burning pot, the kitchen was thick with smoke and the acrid stench of blackened oatmeal made him cough.

"Ah. Lord Gunn. I need to get Miss Carter's breakfast up to her, but I'm afraid the porridge is ruined. There's some toast and pot of tea on the tray though. Would you mind awfully taking it up for me? If you pop it outside her door and knock, no doubt she'll collect it. I'd do it myself only—" Agnes flung the burnt pan into the porcelain sink. It hissed as it hit the cold water.

"Er... certainly." Midnight said, picking up the tray from the table. "Once more unto the breech, I suppose."

"Sorry?"

"Nothing. I'll take it to her now, and then I must go. I'm riding into Edinburgh and will most likely be away until supper."

"Oh. Well then, I'll save you something," she offered.

Chancing a glance at the still-hissing pot, he replied. "No need, thank you. I shall eat in the town."

Agnes gave him a nod and set her mind to the unenviable task of scrubbing the burned pan.

Midnight took the tray upstairs, he met Polly on the landing.

"Is that for Laura?"

"It is," he replied.

"Good, 'cause she's hungry."

"Been for a visit, have you?"

"Yeah. I don't think she's *sick* sick, if you know what I mean? She seems sad is all."

Sad, he thought. *Dear Lord, what have I done?* The tea tray slipped in his hands, and he almost dropped it.

"You alright, Papa?" Polly asked, a look of concern on her cherubic face. "'Ere, lemmie take it." She reached for the tray, and he let her take it from him. Balancing it precariously between her one good hand and the other side resting on her ruined forearm, she turned and walked the few steps down the landing towards the maid's room then glanced back at him. "Would you knock for me?"

"Of course." He reached the door in two strides and gave an inquisitory knock.

"It's only me," Polly piped up in her best cheery voice. "I got breakfast."

There was a rustling of sheets from behind the closed door and then a soft 'Just a minute, Miss' before the door opened to reveal the housemaid in an all-too-inappropriate state of undress; her long cotton nightgown hung loose, as did her hair, unbraided and let down in all its curled glory.

"Oh!" Midnight and Miss Carter exclaimed together. Polly held up the tray, but nobody noticed. Midnight stared wide-eyed as Laura hastily clutched a hand around the V-neck opening of her nightgown. She hurriedly shifted the bulk of her body behind the door so that only her head was peeking out. Midnight mentally shook himself out of his stupor and turned his back in a vain attempt to preserve the lady's dignity.

"Miss Carter, I do apologise. I should not have dared,

had I known." He spluttered his apology feeling like a complete fool.

"Shall I bring it in, then?" Polly asked

"Pop it on the table, there's a good gal." She waited until Polly was all the way inside before she spoke again in an earnest whisper. "I'm sorry, your Lordship. I had no idea you was outside, else I would've tidied meself up a bit."

"Um. How are you feeling?" Midnight replied, not knowing what else to say.

"Fine. Just a bit under the weather. I ain't used to all the fresh air, I 'spect." Her mildly humorous response was endearing, and Midnight appreciated her attempt at glossing over the awkwardness that now lay between them.

"Well," he said, folding his hands behind his back and rising up on his toes, "I do hope you'll be back with us soon before Miss Carmichael accidentally poisons us all. Or burns down the cottage around our ears."

"Is that—?" Miss Carter paused to sniff the air.

"Burnt breakfast? Yes. You got off lightly with tea and toast, Miss Carter."

"P'raps I'll feel a little better by supper time, eh?"

"Perhaps."

There was silence then until Polly emerged back on to the landing. She looked at her father and the maid then back at her father and grinned.

10

EDINBURGH

Riding Samson had proved quite a struggle at first. The big horse had been most reluctant to be saddled and had made every effort to bite Charlie as he'd attempted to bridle the brute. Midnight had intervened eventually, stroking the horse's withers to send calming light into the quivering flesh.

The first few miles along the Edinburgh road had almost seen Midnight thrown into the brush as Samson jerked and tossed, trying his best to launch the strange man from his back. Midnight carried no crop with which to whip the horse and so he'd decided on letting the animal have his head. They'd galloped at speed, tearing along the dirt road until Samson brought himself down to a comfortable trot, and that's how it had remained, much to Midnight's relief, until he reached the outskirts of the city. Not exactly a 'horse' person, Midnight had to admit that he'd enjoyed the feel of the powerful animal beneath him. The sense of freedom as they'd flown through glen and over hill had been exhilarating. Samson was headstrong, but Midnight felt that he and the horse had reached a certain level of understanding over the course of their journey. Perhaps he might offer to buy him from his cousin... *if she's still alive.*

With Samson safely hobbled at the city stables, Midnight caught a cab into the centre. His first order of business was to visit Mr. Gavill of Rosemont and Gavill. The second was to pay Inspector Anderson a visit for updates on the search for Ms. Adams. There had been no sign of the promised search party on the road that Midnight had seen. He could only conclude that either she had been found—alive or dead—or that more important police business had taken precedent. Either way, he must find out what was happening.

"*Cnoc Sithe*? What does it mean?" Midnight asked, eager to know more.

"Well," replied Mr. Gavill, "it is of course in the Gaelic, and translated, it simply means 'fairy hill'. I presume the property in question is situated on or near a hill?"

"Yes, at the foot of one. There is a stone circle at the top," he added.

Gavill smiled indulgently. "Indeed. A superstitious race, we Scots, though not very inventive when it comes to naming houses. Fairy hills and the like are quite common here, Lord Gunn. The locals will have you believing that house belongs to the wee folk if you're not careful." He chuckled. "Now, I will certainly look into the matter for you, but it might take me a while to trace the legal owner of the estate. How long will you be staying at Samach Cottage?"

"The rest of the summer. You can send correspondence to the cottage or to Glenhaven. Either will do. Thank you."

"Not at all, sir. I hope to have some news for you soon. You can imagine that with the tragic loss of Mr. Rosemont, my workload has doubled overnight, but I shall do my very best." Sadness clouded his eyes and his smile faded. The solicitor suddenly looked old and weary.

"Again, my deepest condolences for your loss. How long had you been partners, if I may be so bold as to ask?"

"Twenty-three years. Evelyn was a true friend as well as a business partner. He and his lovely wife, Janet, proved a great comfort to me after my own beloved passed nigh on twelve years ago now." He heaved a shaky sigh. "I suppose I must now return the favour. Although, I'll be damned if I know what I'm to say to the poor woman."

"Has there been any news? What have the police said about the disappearance, have they any clue?"

"No news. It is the strangest of happenings, is it not? It's as if his body just up and walked out by itself." The old solicitor shook his head in consternation.

Midnight's brow furrowed. It wouldn't be entirely unheard of for a supposed corpse to suddenly reanimate; misdiagnosed death wasn't common, but it did happen. Could Rosemont be one of those lucky ones? Of course, that didn't explain why he was still missing. If he had indeed awoken to find himself on a cold slab, why had he not returned home or contacted anyone? *Amnesia?* No, such a notion could not be entertained when Midnight thought back to the mangled, bloody remains of the body in the alley. There could be no question of survival. The fact that Midnight had not sensed any of the dead man's memories still bothered him. The whole situation made no sense at all.

Gavill cleared his throat, startling Midnight from his internal musings. The solicitor glanced at his pocket watch in a somewhat deliberately subtle way as to prompt Midnight to wonder just how long he had been lost in his thoughts.

Thoughts of the living dead dominated his mind even after his visit with Inspector Anderson. No news of missing corpse Rosemont and no news of Midnight's missing cousin either. Upon enquiry, Midnight had discovered that Anderson and his team had been unable to conduct a further search that morning due to two further killings by the Leith docks.

"It appears we have an entire pack of rabid dogs roaming the area. It's the only explanation for the rate and locations of the attacks. I suspect it began with a stowaway from a foreign ship. My team are scouring the city and dockyards now in an effort to drive them out of whichever pit they're hiding in. If word spreads about a bunch o' blood-crazed beasties, it'll be chaos on the streets!" Anderson had said.

The information was worrying. Midnight had come to Scotland to escape the memory of one such blood-crazed beastie, and now he found himself under the threat of a possible pack of them. And then there was the matter of his cousin. He knew her carriage had been attacked by something dastardly, and he'd encountered Bobby Mac's Barghest himself, as had Polly—the memory made him shudder—but neither he nor his daughter had suffered actual injury. Knowing the strength, size and clear malevolent nature of the creature, it could have—nay, *should have* torn them both to pieces without hesitation, and yet it hadn't.

Midnight's pondering came to an abrupt end as he approached the city's stable yard. Shouts and fervent neighs emanated from the direction of Samson's stall. He quickened his pace wondering just how much damage the crazed horse had managed to inflict upon the unsuspecting stable hands. The scene that greeted him could, upon reflection, be described as quite comical.

"Bastard horse! Wheesht and keep the heid ya d'eil!" cried one man as he swished a bucket in the general direction of Samson's gnashing teeth whilst helping up another unfortunate victim who was sprawled face down in the hay. No less than three other lads surrounded the horse, all with their arms spread wide in a protective corral in a vain attempt to steady the wild-eyed stallion. Samson reared up, pawing at the air with his front legs and squealing in anger.

"Bathsheba's backside!" Midnight cursed and hurried towards the ruckus.

The head hand noted his approach and his face flooded with relief. "Thank Christ, sir. He's fair in a stramash. We dinnae know what to do wi' him," the man said apologetically.

"Don't worry about it. It's nothing you've done. It's just in his nature, I think."

"He needs breaking in properly, that one," said the man wielding the bucket. "I'm fair puckled. He's a soul as black as the Earl of Hell's waistcoat, that one. I'm no' sure he'll let ye ride him hame, sir."

Looking at the frenzied horse, Midnight was inclined to agree. However, home he must go and by hook or by crook, Samson would be his ride. Midnight would not be beaten by a four-legged devil. He at least had that in common with his cousin.

"He will. He'll calm down once we get going." Midnight's conviction wasn't enough to quell the sidelong glances the stable hands exchanged with each other. "Just needs a firm hand is all."

"Needs a bite on the ear, if ya ask me, aye," one of the men muttered.

Midnight held out his palm and made a gentle shushing sound. He approached the flailing horse slowly but assuredly, feeling for the horse's centre, trying to catch his eye.

"Be careful, sir. Something's got him riled, for sure."

"Aye, nae wonder with what's going on in the toon. Animals can sense evil."

Word travels fast, thought Midnight. Inspector Anderson wouldn't be pleased.

Samson tossed his head and snorted, he stamped his feet on the cobbles and gave Midnight a threatening stare.

"Bite me, and you'll find I bite back," he warned the horse in a soft but firm voice. He continued to talk to the beast in hushed tones until he had calmed enough for Midnight to reach out and stroke Samson's withers, once again sending healing energy to soothe him. In a matter of minutes, the big stallion had calmed and stood softly snorting as if nothing had happened.

"Well, I'll be damned," the head hand exclaimed. "You've a fair way with horses, sir. A born equestrian, I'd say, aye."

"Oh, I wouldn't say that. It's just that Samson and I have an understanding of sorts. Don't we, boy?" He turned to the animal and patted his neck then leaned in and muttered in his ear, "Remember, you're not the only one with teeth."

The ride home was far easier than their morning trip. Samson tugged experimentally at the reins a few times in the beginning, as if to test the convictions of his rider, but he soon desisted when Midnight, unperturbed by the attempts to dismount him, managed to satisfy the horse's need to ensure the worthiness of the virtual stranger on his back. Their mutual—although still somewhat wary—understanding stood firm, and both horse and rider made it back to Glenhaven without further incident. That was until they reached the stable yard, whereupon Charlie came hurtling towards them at such a pace and waving something so frantically at them that Samson took immediate offence.

He promptly reared up in protest, dumping the unprepared Midnight, arse first, unceremoniously on the ground. The slighted beast gave both him and Charlie a scathing look and took himself into the stables.

"That blasted horse *is* the devil incarnate," Midnight hissed after him as Charlie bent, full of apology, to assist his master.

"Sorry, sir. I didn't mean to startle 'im. It's just that I knew you'd want to know straight away."

"What is it, Charlie? Is it Polly?"

"No, sir. It's Ms. Adams. She's back! Came trotting up the road riding Gorgon about an hour ago, bold as you like."

"Thank you, Charlie. I'd better go over to the house right away and check on her." Midnight brushed himself down and started towards the main house, but Charlie thrust something into his hand. It was a telegram.

"There's this, 'n' all. It's from London. Marked urgent too, is it."

"So I see," said Midnight, ripping open the telegram. His brows drew together in concern as he read the contents. "Blast it!" he cursed, and shoved the paper back at Charlie.

"Bad news then, eh?"

"Bad timing, certainly." Midnight paused to think, pinching the bridge of his nose between thumb and forefinger. He still had no access to a carriage until Ms. Adams's was repaired, and he could hardly ride Samson back into the city and leave him at the stables indefinitely. "Charlie, you said Ms. Adams was riding Gorgon? Was the horse uninjured? Is he fit to ride?"

"Yeah, I suppose so." Charlie shrugged.

"Right. Saddle him up for me, will you? I'm afraid you'll

need to ride pillion with me into the city. I need to leave for London as soon as possible, and you'll have to bring the horse back here."

"Leave, sir? Is everything right at 'ome?"

"Yes and no. Urgent business, and it really cannot wait. I should only be away a few days, no more than a week, I hope. Saddle Gorgon, and then take him to Samach Cottage, and wait for me there. Please have Miss Carter pack a bag... Actually, no." He paused, remembering his housemaid was ill. "Ask Miss Carmichael instead. I shall go and check on my cousin and return to the cottage forthwith."

"Right you are, sir," said Charlie and trotted off into the stables, leaving Midnight to make his way to the main house.

Craigson answered on the fourth ring. A slight but noticeable crease between his eyebrows belied his carefully controlled countenance. "Lord Gunn. My mistress—"

"Yes. I heard. I must see her before I go." His insistent tone inferred he was not to be deterred, and Craigson stepped back to allow him entry.

He escorted Midnight to the parlour door then hesitated. "Forgive me, sir. I should check to see if my lady is fit to receive guests. She was..." He paused, searching for the right words. "...a little distracted upon her return."

"Of course," Midnight agreed. Although eager to see his cousin, he had learned, after his embarrassing doorstop encounter with his unprepared housemaid, that an unannounced visit was probably not a good idea. He waited, a tad impatiently, for the butler's return.

After a few moments, the door opened and Craigson proffered a gracious half-bow before stepping aside to indicate permission to enter.

Midnight hadn't known what to expect when he laid

eyes upon his cousin, but he was sure that whatever it might have been, it surely wasn't this.

"Greetings, dear cousin. To what do I owe this unexpected pleasure?" Her voice, although clear and unencumbered, sounded monotone and flat.

Midnight's concern grew. He was momentarily lost for words. His eyes passed over her person for signs of physical injury of which he saw none. "Ms. Adams. Are you well? We've all been terribly worried."

"Why, of course. I am quite well, thank you." She smiled a humourless smile.

Midnight reached her in three strides and took her by the elbow. "Madam," he said with said with more force than he intended, "you have been in a serious accident and have been missing for days. You *must* tell me what happened to you and where you have been." It was not a question.

Felicity turned her face to his, a placatory expression fixed in place. "Your concern for my welfare is admirable indeed." She touched a gloved hand to his cheek. "In truth, I am struggling to reconcile my feelings with the trauma that I have endured these past few days. Forgive me, cousin. I owe you the truth. But please, allow me time to settle in, and I will tell you my sorry tale in my own time." Pleading eyes met his, and his resolve crumbled.

He immediately regretted his initial insistent manner. Of course, she would need time to recover from what must have been a harrowing experience. He was relieved to observe that she suffered no apparent physical injury, but he had failed to account for any damage to her psyche. Cousin or not, she did not owe him any explanation that she did not wish to give. They hardly knew each other, after all. Inspector Anderson, however, was a different matter.

"It is I who should beg forgiveness, cousin. My concern

overrode my compassion for a moment. As I said, we have all been worried for your safety. Time is something I can give you, however. I must this moment leave for London. Urgent business calls me home. I should be away no more than a week, but I fear I must beg a favour of you, although you may be in no state of mind to acquiesce."

"Ask away. I shall endeavour to do my best."

"My intention is to return to Scotland as soon as my business is concluded. It is my wish that my household remain at Samach Cottage until then... if that is agreeable to you? I regret that I must abandon you in your time of need, but my staff may help in my stead. Charlie has been most useful in the stable yard whilst your man McDonald is recovering, and I can ask my housemaid to attend to you during your own recovery if you need her."

Ms. Adams turned to face the window. She took her time to answer.

"It would appease my conscience, cousin, knowing that you were not convalescing in solitude." His appeal worked for she turned to him with a thankful smile and a grateful nod.

"Then I feel it my duty to agree, since it is my own worrisome absence that has caused you such distress. I would be most grateful of the company. I shall go one better and insist that your household move into Glenhaven with me until your return. That way we can all keep an eye on each other, yes?"

"Well, I... suppose—"

"Good. It is decided then. And now you must off away to London and leave us all to sit in desolation without you." She pouted.

Midnight considered her for a moment. Something about the situation bothered him, but he could not put his finger on it and time constraints would not allow him to dwell on it either. Ms. Adams was right, he must away home immediately and without delay. "If you are sure?"

Ms. Adams inclined her head. "Absolutely."

"In that case, I will send word with Charlie to have everyone move to the house by this evening. That way Miss Carter and Miss Carmichael can assist you in settling back in. I wish you well, cousin. We shall converse again in a week." Midnight took his leave, relieved at his cousin's reappearance but awash with concern and a distinct feeling of unexplainable unease.

11

UNWELCOME INDENTURE

"Whe

"When will he write, Laura? It's been three whole days now and we ain't heard a bleedin' word."

"Hold your tongue, young lady. Ain't no place for foul language in this 'ouse." Miss Carter scolded Polly as she tucked her into bed. "Besides, ain't no cause for the master to write. 'E'll be back soon enough. Did you wash behind your ears?" Polly rolled her eyes and nodded. "Hmm. Now be a good girl, and wait for Miss Carmichael to come read you a story, all right?" Miss Carter patted the girl's cheek and turned to go.

"Do you miss 'im?"

Polly's words halted the housemaid's steps for the briefest moment, but it was enough to set Miss Carter's heart pounding inside her chest. "Goodnight, little miss," she said in as much of a controlled manner as she could muster. She closed the bedroom door and leaned against it, taking a deep breath. How was it that such an innocent question could cause such a violent response inside of her?

If the truth be told, she didn't know how she felt about her master being away—something akin to relief, she supposed. With him not around to remind her of that awful night when he had held her hand, she could at least get on with her duties and try to put the incident from her mind, although that was proving most difficult. She groaned. *What must he think of me?*

Advancing footsteps extracted her from her thoughts. It was Polly's governess come to read the little miss her usual bedtime story.

"Evening, Miss Agnes. She's all tucked in and ready for you."

"Thank you, Laura. Although, I fear it shall be a brief session this evening. I feel very tired."

"I'll away and see to her ladyship now then. Let you get on wiv it. Goodnight."

"Goodnight."

Laura steeled herself in preparation to attend to her nightly duties to her new, albeit temporary mistress. Her first port of call was the kitchen where the cook, Eunice Wick, a thoroughly dislikable rotund woman in her mid-forties, would have a supper tray ready for her to take back upstairs for Ms. Adams. 'Wicked Wick'—aptly named by Laura— since discovering the young housemaid's fear of all things canine, would gleefully anticipate the nightly visit ensuring that the Glenhaven 'Hell Hounds'—as Laura referred to Faolan and Artair—would be neatly ensconced by the kitchen hearth upon her arrival. The ruddy-faced pastry puff would place the tray on the far corner of the kitchen table, knowing that Laura must pass by the dogs to retrieve it.

"Evening, Mrs. Wick. I've come for her ladyship's tray."

Laura's eyes went straight to the table where she anticipated the tray would be.

"Ah, Miss Carter. Here you are at last. I was afeared my mistress's supper would go cold you've taken so long. I've put it on the table, there." She nodded to where Laura was already staring.

"Of course you did." Laura sighed. A low growl emanated from the hearth, she did not look there, but kept her focus on the supper tray, walking steadily yet determinedly towards it. Another growl joined the first, and her knees began to shake just a little.

"They can sense fear, you ken," Wicked Wick said in spiteful triumph.

"Yes, so you keep tellin' me," Laura replied through gritted teeth. She reached the far corner of the table and grabbed for the tray. Faolan rose, snarling. Laura pulled the tray towards her and hugged it to her chest to stop it from shaking then backed away from the two dogs, taking care not to look them in the eye.

"Be sure and bring the empties back doon for bedtime."

"Yes, Mrs. Wick." Laura scurried from the room cursing under her breath.

Her earlier relief at her master's absence was quickly replaced with annoyance at it. Not for the first time did she wish she was back at the little cottage away from stinking Ms. Adams and her stinking stupid staff. Laura's dislike for the lady of the house had been instant. Her constant fawning over her 'dear kind cousin' and his generosity in lending her his staff got right on her nelly. Better still would be to be back at Meriton House with kindly Mr. Morgan and lovely Mrs. P.

Felicity Adams's boudoir occupied almost the entire upper west wing. A huge oak door opened into the large private sitting room. From there one entered the dressing room with a small ante-chamber that housed her private bathroom. The bedroom could be accessed via a set of double doors just right of the dressing room. The fire was lit in the sitting room, but the double doors were closed.

Laura balanced the supper tray on one arm and knocked.

"Entré" came the weak and muffled voice from beyond.

Laura rolled her eyes and turned the door handle. She plastered her most pleasant smile on her face and entered as instructed. "Supper, ma'am. Nine o'clock, as requested." She plopped the tray down on the bedside table and bobbed a polite curtsey.

Ms. Adams stole a look at the small dresser clock. "Mais non, mon petite souris. Il est neuf heures passées. Tu es en retard," Ms. Adams bemoaned.

Laura gave her an impatient sideways look. Another reason she did not like being in service to this mistress was her insistence on speaking 'fancy'. The woman knew she did not speak French but seemed to take great pleasure in teasing her with it nonetheless. Ms. Adams smiled weakly at her and waited.

Laura sighed and played the game. "Beggin' your pardon, ma'am, but I ain't rightly understanding your mean- ing... as you know." The last bit was muttered under her breath.

"Ahh, of course. I keep forgetting. I once had a French maid you know, El—"

"Elise," Laura interrupted, protocol going out of the window along with her patience. "I know, ma'am. From Bacarpooey." ,

Ms. Adams tittered and corrected her pronunciation. "Bacquepuis, dear girl. I must have words with my dear cousin when he returns. Perhaps he can have the lovely Miss Carmichael give you some instruction, hmm? She speaks perfect French. Milk first, please."

Laura put down the teapot and swapped it for the milk jug, sorely tempted to empty it over Ms. Felicity Fancypants.

With her duties done Laura's annoyance dissipated a little but not enough that she felt like she could sleep. She made her way down to the stable yard in search of Charlie. Miss Carmichael was pleasant enough, but she seemed quite enamoured with the mistress of the house, and Laura didn't think she would understand her frustrations. No, she needed someone on her own level, someone down-to-earth like Charlie.

It was almost fully dark outside with the first faint glint of a star waiting to shine. The sky was clear, the air fresh and sweet-smelling. This was the one thing about Scotland that she liked better than London, its distinct lack of smog. The sweet air became tinged with another smell soon enough. The sour tang of manure penetrated her nostrils as she approached the stables causing her nose to wrinkle in distaste.

"You there, Charlie? It's only me." She waited a moment and ventured further into the yard towards the open door. "Charlie?" A noise to her right made her turn sharply, but she could see nothing. "Charlie, that you?" The slight shake in her voice betrayed the silent rumblings of fear that had begun to bubble in her stomach. Laura clutched her shawl tighter around her shoulders as a sudden chill crept over her. She looked around her trying to ascertain the direction of the low grumble that rode on the evening breeze, her first thought being that that cuttleskunk Wick had let the dogs out and the fiends had tracked her down. She kept her back to the stable door and slowly shuffled towards it, her eyes scanning the yard and surrounding brush for any sign of movement. Something brushed her elbow. She screamed and turned to face the oncoming terror.

"What the bleedin' 'ell are you doing 'ere at this hour?"

"Charlie! You scared the blazes outta me. Lord 'ave mercy. I think my heart just stopped."

"Is somefink wrong up at the 'ouse?"

"No. I couldn't sleep is all. I needed a break from it." Laura shrugged, her heart almost returned to its regular rhythm now.

Charlie hooked his arm through hers and led her through the door. "Best come inside, eh? I got a bit of sherry hidden away in the Stable Master's quarters. Fancy a nightcap?"

"Reckon I fancy two after that fright." Laura grinned up at him.

He grinned back at her and winked. "Doing your nut up at the big 'ouse, is it?"

"Just a bit. Her ladyship ain't the easiest mistress, that's for sure, and that old crone-of-a-cook is even worse. She' right got it in for me she 'as. Takes real pleasure in taunting me with them bleedin' hounds. I thought they were going to get me just now. I swear I heard the beggars growling in the yard."

"Yeah, old Eunice lets 'em out for a run near supper time but not usually this late on." Charlie pulled a stool out for Laura to sit on while he reached for a half-empty bottle of sherry. "Only one cup, sorry." He poured some of the alcohol into it and handed it to her.

She smiled gratefully. "Cheers, Charlie."

"Cheers." He replied and took a swig straight from the bottle.

"Never mind, eh? His lordship'll be back soon and then they'll be out of your hair. Mind you, from what Eunice says, Ms. Adams is looking to be seeing a lot more of 'im when he returns."

Laura choked on her drink. A dribble of golden liquid ran down her chin and she hastily scrubbed it away with a corner of her shawl. "What? His lordship and Ms. Fancy-pants? Getting married? That... that can't be right, can it?" She did not like the feeling of sudden anguish that flooded her heart. "I can't, I *won't* work for that woman! I won't Charlie."

He put a calming hand on hers. "Who said anyfink about marriage? Eunice reckons her mistress is just a bit lonely and after a bit of, well, you know—" He cleared his throat, embarrassed.

Laura's mouth dropped open in shocked indignation. The very thought of her and him, *together*, turned her stomach. She gawped, unbelieving, at Charlie who in turn stared back at her his brow creased in confusion. "Why you cryin'?"

"I'm not." Laura spluttered in denial, but a quick hand to her cheek showed otherwise. She wiped the evidence away and sniffed defiantly. "All right, I am. So would you be if you faced the prospect of serving that harlot for the rest of your days! She enjoys flauntin' her fancy-French-fluff in my face all the bleedin' time. Makes me feel stupid. I hate her."

"Well, that's a bit 'arsh in'it? She can't be that bad, been all right wiv me, she 'as. I wouldn't mind 'avin her French fluff in my fa—"

"Oh! Go to 'ell, Charlie Fenwick." Laura rose abruptly, slammed her cup down on the table and stormed out.

It had begun to rain, and by the time she reached her bedchamber, she was soaked to the skin and shivering. Her desolation flowed so deeply, she didn't even bother undressing but merely flopped into her bed, fully clothed, and cried herself into a stupor. Her sobs muffled by the pillow she had clamped over her head, she didn't notice the creak of the floorboards outside of her door.

12

IMPENDING THREAT

"It's been awful, sir. Its voice is in my head all through the night. Mr. Morgan and I, we ain't slept a wink these past few nights." Clementine Phillips stood in front of her master, wringing her hands in her apron, her brow creased in worry as she related her terrifying tale. "First night, I put it down to a bad dream, and then when it 'appened again, I went to the kitchen to make a hot cocoa and Mr. Morgan was already there. Turn' out we had the same dream."

"Only it wasn't a dream."

"No, sir. It was not," Giles replied, stiff-shouldered and chin raised high as if he resented the truth of it.

"Describe to me, as much as you can, what you heard and what you saw." Midnight removed the top from the crystal brandy decanter and poured out three large glassfuls, handing one to Giles and another to a nervous Mrs. P.

"Please, sit." He indicated to the two high-backed chairs by the library fireplace. It was not unusual for him to ask his staff to sit in his presence. They were more like family, and neither of them paused when asked. Mrs. P. looked rather relieved to be off her feet, if the truth be told. The three of them sipped simultaneously, not savouring but relishing the burn as the deep amber liquid soothed their tensions. Midnight stood staring into the cold grate, the glass in his left hand, his right arm resting on the stone mantle as he listened to Giles recount the tale.

"It began in the early hours—the voices. They were indiscernible at first but then we began to understand them." He paused and inhaled deeply before continuing. "They called to us, by name, insisted we come to them. As dear Mrs. Phillips said, that night in the kitchen, the voices became more insistent, loud."

"So loud." Mrs. P. whispered and shivered.

Giles gave her a knowing look before he continued. "We had to look, sir. You understand? We had no choice. And when we did—"

"Ohh!" Mrs. P. gasped in terrified remembrance. "Horses, sir. Big and black they were with yellow eyes and smoke billowing from their nostrils like the devil's own chimney. It was them what spoke to us, 'cept their mouths didn't move at all."

"And what did they want with you?" Midnight enquired.

"For us to come outside," Giles replied.

"But we didn't, sir. I wanted to but Gi—Mr. Morgan, he stopped me. He was so strong, he was. Held on to me so tight." She glanced gratefully at the hero of the hour. "He kept telling me they would go away eventually, and they did... till the next night."

"And what happened the next night?"

"The very same thing. We're at a loss, sir. You know I would not have sent word unless it was urgent, but we just don't know what to do," Giles said apologetically.

"It's fine, Giles. I would not expect you to deal with this

yourselves. Did you find anything in the library?" Midnight asked, knowing full well that Giles would have already searched the extensive collection of occult volumes kept amongst the stacks.

"I did. I think they are 'Pooka', and that's what worried me. The citation states that they inevitably cause disaster when they are ignored."

"Hmm."

"Can you do anything, sir?" Mrs. P. asked hopefully.

"Perhaps. I need to find out what it is they want first. You are sure they didn't say anything significant? Make any demands on either of you?"

"No, sir. We tried to block them out but then we became worried after Mr. Morgan made his discovery. We have no clue why they came."

"I suppose we will find out tonight then, for I predict they will return again until they get what they came for."

It was stifling enough without a fire in the library on a summer's evening. Midnight pored over the entry in the book that Giles had handed to him. He ran a finger around his collar, longing to trade the choking garment for his silk pyjamas. The journey from Scotland had been long, hot, and worrisome.

Pooka - a mythical being of Irish mythology. Known to take many forms, this destructive shapeshifter favours that of a black horse with billowing mane and piercing yellow eyes. Ignore its call at your peril. A Pooka has but one directive: to cause mayhem and mischief. It will seek out and summon victims, lulling them into compliance with its magical ability to

mimic human speech. Once mounted on its back, the Pooka will
embark upon a turbulent journey, carrying its victim far from
home over moor and hill, eventually throwing the afeared rider
from its back before disappearing.

The quarter-hour chime rang from the grand library clock, causing Midnight to look up from his desk.

"Fifteen minutes until the witching hour and I'm still no clearer on how to proceed." He slammed the book shut.

"Perhaps they won't return after all." Mrs. P. looked more hopeful than she sounded.

Midnight shook his head. "I fear it is inevitable, dearest Clementine. If I could only work out their motive, I might know how to banish them for good. I cannot believe that they have targeted this household randomly and for no other reason than to cart you both off and deposit you on some lonely moor."

Mrs. P. let out a tiny squeak of apprehension at this. Giles offered her more brandy, which she took most gratefully and downed in one gulp, making her eyes water with the heat of it. "Then, what are we to do?" she croaked.

"We wait," said Giles. "And when they return, the master will deal with them."

"Your confidence in me is flattering. Let's hope it's not unfounded in this instance."

"You've dealt with worse, sir."

"I suppose I have. Although, I admit to becoming weary of every beast in the book seeking out my company of late."

"There have been others? In Scotland?" Giles enquired.

"The little miss, is she—?" Mrs. P. cut in.

Midnight blew out a breath. "Miss Polly is fine." He tried to sound as reassuring as he could. Telling them of their close encounter with the Barghest was probably not the best idea at present. "It is as you say, Giles. I've dealt with worse. I'll fill you in later. For now, we must prepare for our imminent visitor. I'll go and gather my things from the basement. Giles, check that all the doors and windows are locked, and dear Mrs. Phillips, do stop wringing your hands in your apron, you'll wear a hole in it." He took the housekeepers hands in his own and squeezed them gently.

"What should I do?"

"Fetch salt. As much as you can find. Sprinkle it on the window sills and across the door thresholds. That should prevent them from entering at least."

"Yes, sir." She bobbed her head in acquiescence and toddled off to the kitchen. Giles disappeared to check all the entrances and openings to the house, leaving Midnight to gather his thoughts as he descended the secret stairway from the library into the hidden basement below.

It was here that he kept his amulet, his crystals, and some of his more dangerous occult artefacts not intended for innocent eyes. The amulet in question had last been in use when his daughter Polly had first come into his care. She had seen his dark side and it had frightened her so much that she couldn't bear to be in his presence until the amulet had shielded his horrific face from her. In the past he'd used it to boost his powers but since he'd learned to blend both light and shadow, he'd not had need of it. Now, facing an unknown foe, he thought it couldn't do any harm to harness a little extra power. He gathered to him all of the things he knew to be useful in banishing creatures from the otherworld.

As he ascended the stairs, he heard the chimes ring out above him as the clock struck twelve, and somewhere in the distance, the muffled whinnies of several horses.

13

A SCOLDING

"I will not tolerate loose behaviour in my house, Miss Carter. You seem to think that you may behave how you please now that your master is not here to keep you in check." How Felicity Adams maintained her controlled demeanour whilst flinging false accusations at her was beyond Laura. It was all the young housemaid could do to stand in one place and listen to the lying leasing-monger while she rattled off a list of untruths.

That fetid old kettlescale Mrs-bloody-Wick! I'll get her for this. Nosey old trout. Laura could see 'Wicked-Wick' skulking in the corridor. Every now and again, the hag would peek round the open door to gloat at the result of her tattle-taling. Laura tried to focus her mind on a suitable means of revenge in order to drown out the flagrant lies and insults that poured forth from Mistress Adams's thin-lipped mouth.

"Well, at least you have the good grace to look ashamed. I must say I—"

"What?" Laura's head snapped up. She hadn't realised her gaze had drifted towards the floor but not in shame. She'd been contemplating if the Persian rug was large enough to accommodate the sizeable figure of the cook after she bludgeoned her to death with one of her stale bread rolls. "I ain't ashamed of anything actually." She blurted out before she could stop herself, the colour rose in her cheeks.

Ms. Adams rose from her seat slowly, her tall frame towering over Laura even though there was not much difference in height between them.

Laura bit her bottom lip.

"You were seen coming from the stables late at night. In your nightclothes!" Ms. Adams spat.

"I went for a walk, ma'am. I was hot." Her flush conveyed her innocent protestations as false.

Ms. Adams took it for shame and not the anger that it was. "A floozy and a liar. My, how my dear cousin has been fooled. I shall ensure he is made aware of your true nature upon his return. You are to be put on kitchen duties until that time. Mrs. Wick will supervise your every move."

Laura's blood boiled but she held onto her anger and her tongue and merely gave a stiff curtsey.

"And mark me Miss Carter. I do not generally give second chances. Had you been in my employ, you would be out of a position. Think of this a temporary reprieve as I am quite sure that when Lord Gunn hears of your disgraceful behaviour, he too will feel the same as I."

This was the straw that broke the camel's back. Laura hurried from the room before the tears fell from her eyes and bumped right into the chuckling cook.

"Well, well. Who's been a little harlot then, eh?"

"You wicked old cow. I'll get you for this." Laura promised through gritted teeth.

"Aye? Threats now, is it? I'm sure the mistress would be verra pleased to hear it."

"Don't you dare!" Laura stamped her foot.

Wicked Wick puffed out her copious chest and drew up her many chins. "Oh, I dare lassie. In fact, I'd take great pleasure in it, ya wee fraoch. Now, stop your haverin' and get back to work. There's a kitchen floor to be scrubbed." She grinned in a most sadistically satisfied manner before barging past Laura, whose tears now fell unchecked. They plopped onto the polished parquet floor in large droplets of sheer frustration.

HER HANDS STUNG where the soap penetrated her cracked fingers. Laura had been on her knees scrubbing the vast kitchen and scullery floors for hours. Under the scrutiny of old Wick and the hell-hounds, her hands had barely been out of filthy water all day, but she refused to give the old besom the satisfaction of seeing her discomfort. She'd even hummed a song as she worked until ordered to stop under threat of an angry cook and snarling dogs. It came as a huge relief when she finished the last corner just before supper.

"Empty your pail outside, rinse it oot—and the brush and rags too. They'll dee for another day I'll have no waste in my kitchen. Hurry up aboot it too, lass. You've the mistress's tray to take up afore nine."

Laura scrambled stiffly up from the cold stone and hauled her pail out to empty it in the small kitchen court-yard. There was a water pump and bucket where she could wash out the rags and a line where the cloths could be pegged out to dry. It was as she was pegging out the rags that she heard a small but very insistent '*psst!*' Her eyes widened at the sight of bobbing brown curls under a white cap and a pair of gleaming eyes peering at her from around the corner.

"Miss Polly? What are you doing out here? Ms. Carmichael will have a fit if you get your dress dirty."

"Nah, she won't. It was her what sent me." The little girl popped out from her hiding place and skipped merrily over to her. She flung her arms around the housemaid and squeezed. "Aggie told me everyfin'. She heard the mistress shouting at you from the hall, said she was right 'orrible to you and that you'd been sent to the kitchens. Means we can't sup wiv you no more, least not till Papa comes back anyway."

"No, I'm afraid not, Miss Polly." She didn't want to think about what Lord Gunn would say about the matter. She supposed it would depend on who he got the story from first —Ms. Adams or Miss Carmichael. "But why have you come here? Shouldn't you be getting ready for your supper and bed little miss?"

"I got somefin' for ya, ain't I! 'Ere." Polly shoved a small glass bottle into her hands.

Laura held it up to read the label. "Syrup of figs. What do I need this for?"

Polly stifled a giggle. "Aggie keeps it in her medicine chest, gives it to me sometimes when I can't go to the lav." Her eyes shone with mischief.

"Right," Laura replied, full of suspicion, "and what exactly am I meant to do wiv it?" she asked but had a sneaking feeling she already knew the answer.

Polly shrugged nonchalantly. "It's mushroom soup for supper. I'm sure you'll fink of somefin'." She grinned and ran off.

Laura stared at the bottle in her hand. Dare she do it? If she got caught, it would surely cost her her position. She'd need to be careful. She slipped the bottle into her skirt pocket and returned to the kitchen, empty pail in hand but her heart full of glorious rebellion.

"MISTRESS! Mistress! Stop! Don't eat it." Wick came bumbling up the stairs towards Laura, who was on her way down after delivering Ms. Adams a most delicious supper.

She tried her very best to wipe the smirk from her face but the cook caught it and grabbed hold of her wrist in a vice-like grip.

"You evil little—! Come with me you wee walloper." Wick dragged the struggling housemaid back up the stairs to Ms. Adams's suite.

"Let go of me!" Laura demanded as she tried to prise herself loose to no avail.

The pair of them burst through the double doors to face the startled and rather miffed-looking lady of the house.

"Wick? What is the meaning of this? Is it too much to ask to have my supper in peace?"

"Do not eat that soup!" Wick yelled.

Ms. Adams blinked once, obviously not used to being yelled at by her staff. Something about the cook's expression stopped her and instead of chastising the pair of them for their rude interruption, she obeyed and put down her spoon. "Someone better tell me what on Earth is going on and fast. I am tired and in need of nourishment."

"Beggin' your pardon, ma'am, but how much of the soup have you eaten?"

"Why? What's wrong with it?" Felicity shrank back from her supper tray as if she'd suddenly been served a dish full of adders.

"It's poisoned!" Wick said dramatically and thrust the little glass bottle in the air for all to see.

Laura gasped inwardly and used her free hand to pat her skirt pocket where she'd returned the empty bottle after mixing the syrup into the soup. Her pocket was empty.

Ms. Adams gasped, a hand shot to her chest, and she glared at Laura with all the venom she could muster. "Youuu! You dared to poison my food? You ungrateful little wretch. I should have you flogged for this!"

"It ain't poison. It's medicine," Laura protested, still struggling against Wick's death grip.

"Liar!" Ms. Adams shouted. "I shall have you arrested for attempted murder. You're going to prison and you're going to rot there."

"Maybe even hanged, aye?" Wicked Wick cut in spitefully.

"No!" The shout came from the open door and Polly came hurtling in, tears streaming down her cheeks. "Leave 'er alone! She ain't done nuffin'. It was me. I did it." Polly went straight for Wick and kicked her right in the shin.

The cook let out a squawk and let go of Laura who gathered Polly to her and staggered backwards unsure of her next move.

"Craigson! Craigson!" Ms. Adams shouted her butler, who appeared within moments, huffing, and panting after running up the stairs.

Wick and Ms. Adams were circling Laura and Polly, their arms outstretched to prevent escape. Polly was openly sobbing and muttering a thousand stuttering apologies to Laura, who tried her best to calm the shaking child. She had no idea what to do now. She had never thought things would get so out of hand.

She held out a pleading hand to the mistress. "It ain't

poison. I promise ya. It was just a joke is all. I meant no 'arm. Just intended to give you a bit of bellyache, eh? Nuffin' serious like. I shouldn't have done it. My apologies, ma'am." What else could she say? She was not prepared to go to prison or worse, hang for it.

"Craigson. Send an urgent message with the stable lad. Tell him to fetch the police immediately. There's been an attempt on my life." Craigson looked stunned but nodded. "Then come back here and restrain this woman." Craigson turned on his heels and ran down the corridor to find Charlie. Ms. Adams suddenly doubled over in pain, clutching her stomach. Wick dropped her guard.

"Run!" Laura shoved Polly towards the door. Polly ducked under Wick's arm as she recovered too slowly and made a clumsy grab for the girl. Laura barrelled into her with her whole body, causing the fat old trollop to tumble on her well-rounded behind. The pair of them ran out of the door and down the stairs as fast as their feet would carry them. They heard a muffled shout from above.

"Craigson! Unleash the hounds!"

Laura's heart skipped a beat. She had no chance of outrunning those dogs. "Keep going, Polly!" she panted. "Go find Charlie. Hurry." They made it through the big front door and into the driveway. "Go!" Laura yelled. Polly ran around the side of the house towards the stables whilst Laura ran in the opposite direction. If she could make it into the woods, she might have a chance and at least Polly would be safe from the dogs with Charlie.

She was fifty yards from the edge of the estate boundary when Faolan and Artair leapt out from the brush to her right, teeth gnashing and snarling, dog spittle dripping from their bared fangs. Laura screamed and stumbled backwards right into the grip of Craigson.

"Come quietly miss and nobody gets hurt."

Laura struggled against him, the hounds nipping at her ankles. She squealed again and lifted one leg to avoid Artair's snapping jaws. Faolan took that as a threat and sank his teeth into her calf. Craigson's shout of 'release' was drowned out by Laura's scream of pain. She went limp in the butler arms and allowed him to drag her back to the front steps where a furious Felicity Adams and a gloating Wicked Wick waited. Laura felt dizzy. The pain in her calf was excruciating. She could feel blood trickling down her leg and into her shoe. Still, she managed to stand, defiant in defeat, to face her enemies.

"You insubordinate wench. I will make sure you pay dearly for your disobedience. You will wait inside. Craigson, lock her in the scullery until the police arrive."

Craigson took her by the arm and led her up the stairs. Charlie and Polly came hurtling around the corner at the same time as Agnes Carmichael emerged from the front door, mouths agog at the scene before them.

"Miss Carter?" Agnes questioned. "What on Earth has happened?"

"Laura!" Polly shouted and ran forwards before Charlie could stop her. "Let her go, you bastard!"

Gasps of horror emanated from the people gathered.

"Polly!" both Agnes and Charlie shouted at the same time.

The slap came out of nowhere. So sudden and powerful it had been that nobody realised what had happened at first until they saw the girl lying on her back on the stone steps.

"I will not tolerate such language from a foul-mouthed skelpie in my house." Ms. Adams demeanour was outwardly calm. It seemed impossible that she had been the one to slap Polly.

Charlie stood in shock, and Agnes stepped forward to help her charge, but nobody had noticed that in the confusion, Craigson had let go of Laura. She only needed that split second of freedom to do what she needed to do.

The young housemaid swung her arm back as far as she could and launched herself at Felicity. Her reciprocal slap echoed like a gunshot in the dead of the night, but it had the desired effect. The lady of the house was sent reeling backwards into one of the stone pillars on the porch.

Laura's leg, and now her hand, stung like buggery but she paid it no mind. The satisfaction of seeing that priggish witch on her backside overrode it. Her gratification was momentary when the two hell-hounds rallied to defend their mistress and lunged at Laura. Everything happened in slow motion.

Polly stirred and sat up, pressing her stump to her reddened cheek, directly in the path of the two snarling hounds. Their attention switched from Laura to the little girl, seeing her as the nearest threat. Agnes screamed and reached out. Charlie bolted forwards but he was too far away. Craigson yelled, '*HALT!*' But the dogs were baying for blood. Even old Wick looked uneasy. But it was Laura who flung herself towards the two terrors, barreling into the lead dog. Faolan? Artair? She didn't know or care which one it was. She braced herself for impact but something got in the way.

Suddenly she was flying backwards instead of forwards. She landed hard on her bottom, the wind went out of her, and she watched in confused fascination as something large and furry bit down on one of the dogs' neck. The dog crumpled. The shaggy beast dropped it and pounced on the other. Artair. It was Artair, Laura noted. He was facing off a huge wolf-like creature that towered above him. The creature snarled. Artair turned tail and ran.

Then Charlie began yelling and waving his arms around. Why? Sounds were muffled. Her ears were ringing, and she could taste blood in her mouth. Craigson, too, was waving his arms, and Agnes was throwing her shoes at the creature. Why didn't they all just run inside?

The beast turned, and Laura felt the world turn with it. Polly was draped in its gaping maw. She hung lifeless and limp like a broken doll. Laura had a second to register what was happening, and then the beast was gone. And so was Polly.

14

A BARGAIN STRUCK

"Now there are three!" Giles exclaimed.

"One for each of us," Midnight muttered. He touched the pendant around his neck, checking to see if he'd charged it with enough energy. Three black stallions, long, flowing manes billowing in the evening breeze, golden eyes fixed on each of the occupants of Meriton house, stood patiently in the lamplit street below. Two he thought he could've maybe defended against, but three? He wasn't confident, even with his amulet. Giles tapped the iron poker held in his hand against his shoe. Mrs. P. had both hands wrapped around an iron skillet from the kitchen. The Pookas watched them and they watched the Pookas. This stand-off lasted all of five minutes, and then their seduction began.

> 'Midnight Gunn. I call to you.
> Come outside, your debt is due.
> Fabled is your lordly name,
> come outside and play my game.
> Come out, come out, be wild and free.

In exchange for a goodly fee.'

Midnight's head felt fuzzy. He shook it. Turning to his companions, he took note of their glazed expressions. "Giles?" He took hold of the older man by the shoulder and gently squeezed. The butler's glazed look gradually faded, and Midnight could see his focus return. "What did they say to you? Did they make demands?"

Giles cleared his throat. "No. It's the same as before. They just ask me to come outside. And... it makes me want to."

Midnight blew out a frustrated breath and turned to his housekeeper. "Mrs. P? Are you with us? What did you hear?"

Clementine patted her brow with her handkerchief before answering. "The same as before, sir. Demanding I come outside."

"Nothing else?"

"No, sir," they answered together.

Midnight uttered his favourite curse. "Bathsheba's backside."

"And you, sir? What did you hear?" Giles asked, sensitive to his master's mood.

Midnight recounted the verse he had been sung. "So, you see. It is uniquely different from yours," he explained. "They're clearly here for me."

"But why?"

"That, Giles, is the question of the hour." He glanced out of the window to the three Pookas. The middle horse, the one who had spoken to him, stamped its foot impatiently. The song began again.

'Come, come, a debt is due.

Promised is the land from you.
Show yourself, no need to hide.
Come, join me for a ride.'

Activating the amulet, Midnight drew on the light from the oil lamps. Opening the window, he bathed himself in light energy and spoke directly to the creature.

"I have promised you no land. What is this debt you speak of?"

The horse tossed its head and whinnied, smoke plumed from its nostrils.

'Poison is thy nominee,
promised is thy land to me.
A bargain struck on sacred soil,
thy worldly goods are ours to toil'

"Poison?" Midnight muttered to himself.

"Have you any clue as to what they want, sir?" Giles asked.

"They seem to want my land or worldly goods. They appear to be convinced that I have struck some sort of bargain with them. I confess, I have no clue as to their meaning."

"Where 'ave they come from?" Mrs. P. asked.

"Let me ask." He spoke directly to the Pookas next. "From where do you hail? Tell me from whence this bargain was struck and by whom, for it was not me."

'Poison is thy nominee,
promised is thy land to me.
A bargain struck on sacred soil,
thy worldly goods are ours to toil.

Come, come do not tarry,
our destination we must hurry
Failure to comply to instruction,
inevitably leads to your destruction.'

"And suddenly an invitation becomes a threat." Midnight did not like the sound of that. His butler and housekeeper had dropped their makeshift weapons and were making their way towards the door. It was all he could do to stop them, so intent were they on following the pookas seductive song. "Hold!" he cried, his hand on Giles's arm "Giles, man. Hold!" It took them both a few moments to come around this time.

"Their pull is getting stronger, sir. It is too hard to resist." Giles beseeched him. "Poor Mrs. Phillips. I fear she cannot hold out much longer."

"Dammit. Wait here, away from the window, and cover your ears." He added, handing them both cushions to muffle out the sirenesque calls. He stood by the open window once more, this time primed with dark power. "Right then, you Celtic fiends. Let's see what you've got shall we." The shadows roiled around him. He embraced the pinpricks of pain. Dark threats deserved dark power. There would be no blending of shades this night.

The Pookas sensed the change in atmosphere and began stomping and neighing in retaliation.

Midnight opened his palms and sent a torrent of shadows to surround the three equine goblins. They screeched in anger, fighting back by blasting his shadows with dark powers of their own. Smoke tumbled from their mouths and nostrils, choking off his own rippling clouds.

'Heed our warning halfling,

tomorrow shall destruction bring.
You have been warned,
disaster reigns when we are scorned'

They turned to leave.

"Wait! What is your meaning? I demand to know. What destruction?" Midnight was suddenly wary of their threats, thinking of Polly, Giles, Mrs. Phillips... Laura. What if these creatures were to harm them? What was a piece of land to him against the threat of the destruction of those he held most dear.

The Pookas ignored him, continuing on their way.

"I will come out!" he yelled.

"Sir! You mustn't," a frightened Mrs. Phillips protested.

The creatures halted their retreat.

"I will come out as you asked, if you promise to leave my family alone. You will do no harm to them." The middle Pooka turned its yellow eyes on him, considering.

'Your family alone we'll leave,
if to our request you'll cleave.'

It cocked its head in curious anticipation.

"I agree." Midnight shouted down.

"Sir—"

"No, Giles. It is the only way to find out what they want for certain. They have promised my family will come to no harm. They are Fae-born, and therefore, supposedly, a promise cannot be broken. I will be fine," he reassured them. He had to have faith his family would be safe. He would have to tackle these beasts alone. And he would win. He had to.

15

FIGHT OR FLIGHT

Polly was gone, Laura's leg was bleeding, and people were shouting. Charlie helped her up.

"You all right? Can you stand?"

"Mmm" was all she could muster.

There was a commotion on the front porch. Wick and Craigson were fussing over the inert form of their mistress. Wick was tapping Ms. Adams's face. Craigson had ahold of her hand and was stroking it.

"You need to 'ide. Go to the stables now. 'Ide in the 'ay loft till I come get you. I'll saddle the horses and take you to the train station in the morning. You can catch the train back to London."

"What? No, Charlie. What about Polly? We need to find her."

"I know. But what are you gonna do, eh? You saw that thing. We need his lordship 'ere to take care of it. You don't even know what it is or where it's gone," Charlie protested. "You don't even know if she's—"

Laura pulled away from him. "I ain't going to London,

Charlie. I need to find the little Miss now. Send a telegram to his lordship. Tell him to come as soon as possible. But I'm going to find her, and you ain't stopping me."

"But. Your leg," Charlie insisted. "You can't go anywhere in that state."

"I can and I will, Charlie Fenwick. That girl needs me. She ain't got nobody else save the master and he ain't 'ere, is he? I'm going and ain't nobody going to stop me."

"At least let me clean that leg, will ya?" Charlie beseeched her.

Laura glanced over to the front steps where Felicity Adams was beginning to stir. "No time. I gotta go now. Can you stall them?" Laura nodded in the direction of the three people who would now be gunning for her arrest.

"I'll think of somefin'. Go on, then. You'd best get a shift on. And take this." He took off his jacket and placed it around her shoulders. "It might be summer, but you never know when it's gonna rain in this country."

Laura touched a grateful hand to his cheek. "Cheers, Charlie. You're a good friend. I'll get word to you somehow, if... *when* I find her."

"When you do, you'll need this." He plonked a small leather pouch in her hand. It jingled. "Buy a ticket to London soon as you can." Laura nodded. "Now, go." Charlie turned her around and gave her a gentle shove.

Laura hobbled off into the night without a backward glance, following the direction that she had seen the beast flee. She had no idea how she would find it; she only knew that she must. Leaving Charlie, Agnes, the house, and very likely her position in Lord Gunn's household behind, she scrambled deeper into the forest, following deer trails that she could barely make out, stumbling over rock and root.

Her leg burned, and she hoped the bite didn't become infected. The deeper she went, the more she struggled. The dense canopy overhead allowed only minimal light to penetrate and finding her way in the growing darkness was proving impossible. As the last of the summer evening light faded, she saw something.

Crouching low, she stretched out her palm and pressed it into a large depression in the ground. Her whole hand, fingers spread wide, barely covered the canine footprint in the dirt.

"Mary, mother of God." Laura whispered.

This thing was huge. How would she even begin to tackle it if she found it? She was petrified of Glenhaven's dogs, let alone this gigantic wolf creature. It would surely crush her neck as it had done Faolan's. Her hand inadvertently went to her neck. She gulped but gathered her resolve. If there was any chance at all that Polly was still alive—dammit, even if she was dead, Laura owed it her and to Lord Gunn to recover her body for a decent burial. That sweet child would not be left to rot in the animal's lair amongst the decaying bones of sheep. Even if it meant Laura's life, at the least, the child would not be alone in her death. If that rotten cow Felicity-bloody-Adams had her way, Laura would be hanging from her neck by a rope by next week anyway, so she may as well die doing something noble.

As the moon rose in a clear sky, Laura had no choice but to cease her search for the night. A slight breeze rustled through the trees. She drew Charlie's jacket tighter around her torso, glad of the extra layer, not just for the added warmth it provided but because it belonged to a dear friend, and somehow, she felt less alone wearing it. Wrapped in its horsey smell, she could almost imagine she was falling asleep in the hayloft of the stable and not amongst the damp, fusty leaf-litter of the forest floor. Her leg throbbed but she was too exhausted to bother. Perhaps God would be merciful and take her in her sleep.

'*Not yet*' were the last murmurings of her drifting mind.

16

WILD HORSES

Midnight held on for dear life. He wasn't the world's greatest rider, but he'd managed to calm Samson with healing energies to at least make him rideable. The Pookas were a different matter altogether. The equine Fae galloped along at a frightening speed. It was no smooth ride either; they kicked their back legs, tossed their heads, and nipped at each other along the way. Having no saddle or bridle, Midnight clung to his mount until his knees ached and his hands went numb. He dared not channel healing energy, even to himself, for fear of angering the Pooka. Until he discovered exactly what it was that they wanted and how they aimed to attain it, he thought it best to just go along for the ride. Hooves clopped along the quiet cobbled streets of the city with unencumbered abandon. At this time of night there weren't many carriages or pedestrians around, save for the odd drunk on their way home from a tavern, and if they saw anything, they would probably put it down to the beer. Come to think on it, he wasn't even sure he *could* be seen. These were Fae horses, after all, and would most likely be glamoured. Just when his backside became completely numb, his ride slowed to a trot and then to a walk.

Midnight recognised the street by the London docks. He now had an inkling of their destination. "Why have you brought me here?" he asked his ride as it came to a halt outside the almost-finished Saint Francis's Charitable Hospital. He dismounted, adjusted his clothing and brushed himself down of road dust and awaited a reply.

> 'Poison is thy nominee,
> promised is thy land to me.
> A bargain struck on sacred soil,
> thy worldly goods are ours to toil.'

The Pooka's familiar couplet penetrated his mind without any movement of its mouth.

"Yes, yes. So you keep saying," he snapped, his patience almost at the limit. "But what does that mean, 'Poison is thy nominee'? And what bargain? I have struck no bargain with you."

The Pooka's yellow eyes flashed in annoyance, it tossed its head, mane flying wildly. It stamped a hoof as if to emphasis its next words.

> 'A bargain struck as guarantor,
> collect we must, tarry no more!'

"I have struck no bargain and have stood guarantor for no one! I demand to know the meaning of this." Away from Meriton House and his staff, he was ready for the challenge now. The shadows pulsed nearby, eager to be summoned. The meagre glow from the gas-lit street lamps flickered, keen to add to his power. They were on his territory, threatening his status-quo, and he had nobody to defend except himself. He was confident he could make them talk.

His theory was tested as the lead Pooka charged at him, head dipped and tail swishing.

Midnight accepted the shadows and the light an instant too late, and the Pooka barrelled into him at full pelt, hitting him in the midriff and forcing the wind from his lungs. He slammed into the old wooden doors at the entrance to the hospital but had little time to recover as the Pooka reared up on its hind legs, preparing to trample him with the front ones. Midnight rolled sideways, gasping for breath but managing to fling a stream of power from his palm to strike the horse on the ear. It screamed and momentarily ceased the attack. The two other Fae flanked their leader and a trio of Pooka's steadily advanced to aid in the onslaught.

Quickly rethinking both his strategy and his ability to defeat them, Midnight had little time to decide on his next move. They had him pinned against the doors. He could not go forward nor escape away to the side. The stone archway was too deep. His only option was to go backwards.

Turning his palms to the rear, he shot a stream of power into the old wood and blasted it inwards. Stumbling a little as the door gave way, he gathered his feet and ran inside. His escape was brief as the sound of hooves followed him, but it gave him enough time to set a little distance between himself and these pesky Pookas.

When the dust from the blast began to settle, dark smoke replaced it, not from his own power. The thick black tendrils curled from the nostrils of the three Fae who stood stamping and snorting in front of him, ready for battle.

Midnight readied himself. He drew in more of the shadows to increase his power, the light giving way to the dark since he was away from the street lighting now. He would never get used to the sting of absorbing dark power but right now, he welcomed it, for these Fae were gearing up to a hellish fight.

'A deal promised cannot be reneged,
to do so will mean your end of days,'

cried the leader.

Midnight gritted his teeth; these riddles were starting to grate on his nerves. "I've made no deal and instructed no other to do so on my behalf. Tell me who has made you such an offer?" *So I can kick his backside from here to kingdom come!* he thought.

'A gentleman of poisoned song.
Demon born, he wooed nightlong,
'With promises of land for toil.
Gifts he bore on sacred soil,
'A bargain struck, he did offer,
us your land to fill his coffer.'
'The time has come to collect,
acquiesce to clear thy debt.'
'This land be ours by your man's hands,
we claim the rights as things stand.'

The Pooka's song ended with an authoritative snort, causing a puff of smoke to erupt from its nose.

"I say again. I gave no orders to strike any bargain with you or your kind. I will not give up my land. This land is sacred also. Sick people will be treated here. It is a place of healing. There is no *toil* for you here. Leave now and seek the blackguard who made you false promises."

The Fae whinnied angrily and charged forward.

Midnight flung a great stream of dark power at the galloping group which hit them with an audible *boom!* The Pooka to the left of the leader fell sideways with an angry cry. In a flash, it turned from a cantering horse into a squat little man with a bulbous nose whose short legs were flailing around in the air as he struggled to get up from the floor.

Midnight had no time to wonder at the sudden transformation before the other two Pookas were upon him, kicking and lunging with gnashing teeth. Midnight threw out tendrils of power in every direction not knowing if his aim was true. He was struggling to see where his enemies were as their own bilious clouds choked him. His eyes began to sting and stream. A wave of panic struck as his throat began to tighten and close. He gasped desperately for air but only succeeded in inhaling more of the acrid smoke. The first waves of nausea hit and fought to stay conscious. This could not be his end. It could not. He had Polly to care for and the rest of his growing household. What would happen to them all with him gone?

17

WIDDERSHINS

Her eyes wouldn't open. They were glued together by the remnants of her tears. *I'm still alive, then.* Laura brought a heavy hand to her face and scrubbed at the crusty coating. She smelled dirt and heard nearby birdsong. A rustling sound close by caused her to bolt upright.

"Ow!" she cried at the stab of pain in her neck. She must've slept funny.

Peeling her eyes open, she took in her surroundings, remembered her plight with a heavy heart and groaned. "Bleedin' 'ell." Her clothes and hair were wet with early morning dew. A violent shiver coursed through her. Charlie's coat fended off much of the morning's sting, but she'd lain there for most of the night, and the jacket, as she discovered when she attempted to stand, hadn't prevented the cold from penetrating deep into her aching bones.

There she stood, chilled to her core and injured, arms wrapped around herself for comfort more than anything else, not knowing what in the world to do next. The fog in her brain lifted when she caught sight of the giant canine footprint again. Adrenaline coursed through her veins driving out the worst of the chill. Taking a step in the direction of the print, she faltered as excruciating pain shot through her calf and into her groin. A whimper escaped her when she lifted her skirt to inspect her leg.

"Mary, mother of God. No!" Her woollen stocking was caked in blood. The dark stain spread from mid-calf to ankle, and she knew she must clean the wound. She would have to find a burn, both to quench her thirst and to tend to her leg, and then she would resume her search for Miss Polly.

"Ain't no good to anyone in this bleedin' state, Lauraloo," she muttered, referring to herself using the nickname her family had given her. A sudden pang of grief filled her belly. *Family.* She missed her own greatly, but this felt different. This pain was for Miss Polly and for... *him.* Oh Lord, how she missed him this very moment. He would know what to do. He would be far better at searching than her. *He* would never have let that beast take Miss Polly in the first place and now... now he would despise her for allowing it to happen.

"I'm sorry! So sorry." Laura sobbed. Tears brimmed in her eyes, spilling freely to forge wet streaks through the dirt on her unwashed cheeks.

She had no option but to stumble her way along the forest path, following the footprints and listening for the sound of water so she might stop and clean her leg, each footfall sending burning, wracking pain through her savaged limb.

It wasn't too long, perhaps an hour Laura estimated, before she came upon a shallow babbling burn. One thing that Scotland had in its favour was that you were never far away from a stream, burn, or loch. The cold running water on her leg gave her instant, if momentary, relief. She discarded the ripped, bloody stocking, dried her foot and leg with her skirt and bandaged her injury with a strip of fabric torn from her petticoat.

"Well, I ain't no Florence Nightingale, but it'll have to do."

The chill crept back into her bones with the name 'Nightingale'. Hemlock Nightingale, the man, the devil, who had stolen her soul, still haunted her dreams. It was unfortunate that he should share surnames with the infamous nurse and her college of female protégés, several of whom would soon be employed at Lord Gunn's new charitable hospital. Still, she refused to allow his memory to interfere with her life.

"Nightingale!" she shouted at the forest, just to prove that she could.

"*OWOOO!*" came a distant reply.

Laura froze. In an instant, the forest fell silent. Birds stopped singing, even the small scatterings of unknown animals in the bracken ceased. The only sound Laura could hear, besides the gentle breeze through the tree tops, was her own thumping heart. It had to be the beast, for no other woodland animals could make that sound unless—*rabid dogs?* Was it possible that she had stumbled upon one or more of the infected dogs that had reportedly been roaming the hills and killing people? The realisation hit her, and in an instant, she was running *towards* not away from the ominous howl.

There was no pack of dogs. There was only one, the one

that had taken Miss Polly. Convinced this was the beast responsible for all the savage attacks, haunted by the vision of the girl hanging limp and unconscious in its vicious maw, Laura gathered every ounce of strength she had and tore through the forest as fast as her injury would allow. Another long howl caused her to change direction. She veered from the main path and turned towards a large, conical hill ahead. The climb was steep, putting even more pressure on her wound. She felt a new trickle of blood seep through her makeshift bandage, run down her leg, and into her shoe, but she would not, could not, stop her pursuit. As she neared the crest of the hill the dense woodland thinned out to form a small clearing in which stood a large megalithic circle. The sight before her stopped her in her tracks.

The two largest of the stones nearest to her were not in alignment with the rest. Instead of facing broadside out, they'd been positioned barely three feet apart and were turned to face each other forming a small passage into the centre of the circle. It was not this oddity that had stalled her. Laura had never seen such a monument and had no idea if the positioning was odd at all. The thing that had halted her run, that she couldn't take her eyes off of, was the dark shaggy creature that circled widdershins around the two monoliths.

She may not know about ancient monuments or big hairy beasties, but she knew of the old wives tales back in London and dancing, or bounding in this case, anti-clockwise around anything meant bad luck. Her fears were vindicated when, after another bone-tingling howl from the wolf-like creature, the passage between the stones began to glow.

It started as a small, circle of light in the centre of the passage and expanded into a blinding starburst within seconds, causing Laura to shield her eyes. Squinting against the searing light she could just make out the hulking form of the creature. It took one last turn around the stones before coming to a stop directly opposite the passage.

Shifting her weight off her injured leg, Laura took a tentative step forward for a better view. Twigs snapped under her foot eliciting the tiniest gasp from her, but it was loud enough to cause the creature to snap its shaggy head back and pin her with a threatening glare. She held her breath not daring to move. In the ensuing stare-down between herself and the animal, she knew if she made a move, she was likely going to be dead very quickly. Steeling herself for the inevitable attack she made a vow: Laura Carter would go down fighting.

18

WHERE LOYALTIES LIE

Midnight could already feel the flesh under his eye swelling from where a well-aimed hoof had knocked him seven bells sideways. But that was nothing compared to the pain in his spine from being slammed into a stone pillar. He lay in a crumpled, gasping heap trying to force his sluggish mind to form some kind of escape plan. From the uncouth language that emanated from somewhere to his right, he knew that the Pooka who had transformed from horse to fat little goblin was still in that form. That left two Pooka's to deal with. If he could just see enough to make true his aim, he could suffer them to the same fate—hopefully. Of course, this plan all depended on whether he could muster enough strength to summon his power to full force. He'd managed it against Hemlock, but then Polly's life had hung in the balance. Was his current doubt evidence that he didn't hold his own life with the same reverence? Had the last eighteen months of parenthood made him soft? Or was he merely out of practice? He'd certainly not had much call to use his unique abilities since the assumed death of that bastard Hemlock and certainly not since the arrival of Miss Carmichael. Perhaps the suppression of his power had leaked it somehow? *What a damned inconvenient time to find out,* he mused. Pushing himself up to a seated position, he rallied himself.

"Do or die, Midnight, old chap."

This was it, his final push. For Polly and everyone who loved him, he could not allow defeat. With a roar, he thrust himself to a standing position, bearing the agony of the shadows' thousand stings as the dark power tore through his body and exploded in a barrage of vengeance. His strike hit the smaller of the Pookas who, with an audible *POP,* fell to the ground in the form of a wriggling goblin, the same as its previous comrade.

The action drove the lead Pooka into a frenzy, and Midnight had no time to redirect his fire. His shot scraped the side of the Fae but didn't do enough damage to turn it. As the animal was almost upon him, something caught Midnight's eye. Something in the dark upper recesses of the rafters moved. Fast.

As the horse bore down on him, the 'something' left the darkness and landed with admirable accuracy on the Pooka's back. The scream that erupted from the horse's mouth would have curdled the blood of the bravest lion. It reared and bucked in front of him, trying without success to throw off its attacker. What was the thing that attacked?

Midnight struggled to make out a recognisable form amongst the smoke. It was only as it dissipated that he could begin to discern the scene before him. Atop the Pooka was some type of winged creature about the size of a small dog but with big paws that sported extremely vicious-looking talons which were currently doing a wonderful job of turning the Pooka's back into a pin cushion. He couldn't put a name to the being, but it did seem decidedly familiar to him. Midnight ducked to avoid a flailing hoof as the Pooka turned in a frenzied circle and his eyes fell upon the face of—

"A gargoyle!"

Surely this was impossible? Goblins and Barghests, he could accept, but gargoyles weren't living beings. He'd admired the gruesome statues that adorned the old dockside warehouse when he'd purchased it almost two years ago, and of course he knew of the legends behind them. Gargoyles were thought to act as loyal protectors for the buildings they adorned and the people who resided within, but to actually see them *alive* for want of a better word, was amazing, even to a seasoned occultist such as himself. Midnight roused himself from his musings and rallied to aid his saviour. He caught the Pooka's muzzle with a dead-centre strike and *POP!* Both the gargoyle and the squat little goblin man clattered to the floor in a flurry of limbs. The gargoyle bit down on the goblin's forearm then leapt off sideways to enable Midnight to cut off its angry cry of pain with a well-placed boot across its fat throat.

"Now. You *will* tell me everything, or I will kill you."

The Pooka-goblin snarled at him then uttered a strangled whimper as the gargoyle, bearing an impressive set of teeth, came to stand beside Midnight and offered up a menacing snarl of its own. The goblin surrendered with a reluctant nod, and Midnight lifted his foot from its neck.

The defeated Fae sat up, heaved a sigh, and began its story. Which, much to Midnight's visible relief, was not in riddles and rhyme. "You put up a grand fight, your lordship," it said, with a slight Irish lilt. "We almost had ye though."

"Perhaps," Midnight replied. "Now, talk."

"I told no lies. A bargain we struck with a curious fellow

who claimed to be acting as your spokesman showed us your family seal to prove his credibility. We had no reason to disbelieve him." He shrugged.

"The name of this man?"

"I don't remember."

"You're lying."

"Fae do not lie! As you should know."

"Perhaps not but they are known to bend the truth when it suits them."

"And what reason would I have to do that? We were promised land—this land. And we are still empty-handed. I may be persuaded to remember it... for a price." The goblin grinned.

"I will not give you this hospital or any land," Midnight said firmly.

"No, not *give*. A loan perhaps?" The little man was gaining in confidence as his two companions skittered over to join him, their actions eliciting another snarl from the gargoyle. "You are an honourable man, that I can tell. So, I'll make you an honourable offer."

"I make no deals with Fae who try to harm my friends and kill me," Midnight retorted.

"Not kill or harm. Just a bit of mischief is all." The claim caused Midnight to snort with derision. "You've seen what we are capable of. We could help you, help protect this land. Let us stay and work the gardens, and in return, we will offer protection to those who wander there."

"I have protection." Midnight indicated the gargoyle. "Why would I need more?"

"Wouldn't hurt, now would it? We don't ask for much, us Pooka, but we need to work the land and grow things to survive. What say you?"

"How quickly your loyalties turn. The name?"

"Do ye agree to a bargain?"

"Give me the name, and I will agree."

"Hemlock Nightingale."

The goblin's words struck Midnight like an ice dagger to his heart. It was as he had feared for the last eighteen months, Hemlock was alive.

"Do we have a bargain?"

"Yes. We have a bargain," Midnight whispered, thinking that if that dastardly devil was alive, he could use all the protection he could get. "But you must promise to uphold your end of it, no switching loyalties to the highest bidder. If you work my land, you protect all who reside within it. This is my condition. Accept it or die right here and now."

The gargoyle snarled, emphasising the threat.

"Agreed, young lord. We shall protect *all* who reside within." With a wink and a broad grin, the lead Pooka and his two companions disappeared.

19

TEA AND TELEGRAMS

Inspector Arthur Gredge shook his hand, his substantial moustache twitching in a brief smile that did not reach his eyes. "What's wrong? You're supposed to be on holiday."

"How very observant of you, Arthur. Do sit."

Arthur sat down but did not relax.

"Tea?"

"Yes, thank you."

"Biscuit?"

"Can we dispense with the fluff and get to why you've called me here? Something is up. I could tell by the nature of your message."

There was a moment of silence as Midnight placed the cup on the desk in front of his friend. He seated himself facing the inspector, folding his hands together he looked Arthur straight in the eye. "He's back."

More silence followed as an understanding passed between the two colleagues.

"You know for certain?" Arthur asked, reaching for his cup and sipping the hot liquid.

"I do." Midnight preceded to recount the events of the previous night. As he continued, Arthur's eyes grew wider by the second. When he'd finished the tale, he sat back in his chair and waited for a response.

Arthur cleared his throat. "Well, if it was anyone else, I'd have you strung up in a straitjacket and committed by now. Gargoyles, eh? Hmm. Well I never."

"There's more," Midnight said and pushed a telegram towards him.

Gredge leaned forward and picked it up. "Why am I not surprised?" he muttered and began reading. It didn't take him long to skim read the message. When he finished it, he pushed back towards Midnight, took another sip of tea and said, "So, when do we leave?"

Midnight gave a wry smile. "I knew I could count on you, Arthur. We leave with tomorrow morning's early train. Six o'clock sharp. Can you clear it with the Yard?"

"I'll think of something."

"Thank you, truly. It's at times such as these one needs a reliable back up and a fresh mind," Midnight said, genuinely grateful.

Arthur snorted at the compliment and waved it away with a hand. "What have you concluded so far? Any other leads other than little goblin-men-horses?" He said the latter without any hint of a sardonic tone which made him shake his head slightly. The things he had encountered since meeting Lord Gunn had chased the skepticism right out of him.

"Not really, but it strikes me as too much of a coincidence that my daughter should be kidnapped by a rabid beast at the very same time I, and my staff, are accosted by Pookas. Wouldn't you agree?" It was Midnight's turn to sip his tea. Although, at this point he would willingly swap tea for brandy were it not for the need to stay clear-headed and focused.

"Yeah, seems a bit suspect I suppose. Miss Polly is our number one priority, that much is clear. What isn't clear is how in Hell we're going to find her. We should start at Glenhaven, talk to Ms. Adams and her staff first. We'll interview them all separately, see if their stories match up. Then we'll talk to Mr. Fenwick. His telegram doesn't make any sense in truth. Why would your cousin attack your daughter?"

"I confess I am at a loss as to that end. Ms. Adams struck me as an amenable enough woman. I would even go so far as to say that Polly liked her. That was good enough for me."

"Mm," Arthur agreed. He knew the little girl had some abilities of her own and was unusually astute when it came to judgement of character. "And you think that this wolf-creature, the murder of your Scottish lawyer and the kidnapping of Miss Polly are all connected somehow?"

"They have to be. The beast turned up twice at the Glenhaven estate: once, to leave a message or perhaps a warning; and the second time, to take Polly. Not to mention the thing killed Mr. Rosemont through whom I was to purchase land."

"And these Pooka things, they wanted to take land away from you upon the instruction of Nightingale. Seems to me Nightingale and this Barghest creature are both on a mission to relieve you of your land."

"Agreed. However, it is my daughter that I am most concerned for now."

"And I'm sure Nightingale knows that. I'm wondering if he plans to exchange the girl for your land?"

"It's a possibility, but a slim one. If that were the case, would the blackguard not wait until I had purchased more land? Why kidnap my daughter now? He could've had ample opportunity to do so in the last eighteen months."

"Hmm." Gredge tugged at his moustache, deep in thought. "What about this Anderson? I would advise sending him a telegram ahead of our arrival. He can begin investigations, might turn up some leads. In a missing person's case, the first twenty-four to forty-eight hours are crucial."

"He seemed a decent fellow, quick to inform and assist when my cou—Ms. Adams," Midnight corrected himself, reluctant to use familial terms when facing the possibility that she had indeed hurt Polly, "went missing."

"Hold up. Ms. Adams went missing too?"

"Yes." Midnight's brow furrowed. "There seems to be an awful lot of disappearing acts in recent days," he concluded, thinking of the missing bodies from the city morgue. "I have much to tell you, Arthur."

Gredge cocked an eyebrow and pushed his teacup aside. "Best pour me something with a bit more bite then, eh?"

20

FAMILY TIES

Inspector Anderson's office reminded Midnight of the tiny bakery on Petticoat Lane in London—small, excruciatingly hot, and full of smoke, only without the delicious scent of freshly baked bread. Anderson stubbed out his cigar. A cloud of cloying smoke permeated the air, causing Mrs. Philips to cough very slightly. Giles Morgan shifted in his seat. Arthur, Midnight knew, was standing in the corner, leaning against the wall near to the almost insignificant window which was barely open a crack. Midnight resisted the urge to run a finger under his collar, despite the uncomfortable heat. The tiny room was not designed to accommodate more than two people at once and the five that had crammed themselves in it now were feeling the uncomfortable effects. He'd been unable and, in truth, unwilling to prevent Mrs. P. and Giles from travelling back to Scotland with himself and Arthur. Once they'd discovered that their beloved 'Polly Peeps' had been taken, there was no discouraging them, despite Midnight's half-hearted protests at the length and arduousness of the journey. They were as much part of Polly's family as he was and therefore entitled to the same concern.

"I cannae allow yous all to come along. You know that, aye?" Anderson said. "This is now an official police investigation. But I cannae exactly stop you from returning to Samach Cottage either. Ms. Adams hasn't rescinded her invitation to stay, I take it?"

"Not thus far. Although things might change once we start to question her."

"*I* shall do the questioning, Lord Gunn. No disrespect to you, but you're far too emotionally involved."

"And no disrespect to you, *Inspector,* but Lord Gunn is under my command as an official consultant for Scotland Yard." Gredge cut in.

Anderson narrowed his eyes, clearly put out by the intrusion on his patch by a 'Yardy'.

"Scotland Yard is no Scotland. My town, my rules."

Midnight caught the twitch in Gredge's moustache and cut in before tempers rose. "Forgive me, Inspector Anderson. Can I ask why you allowed me to accompany you in the search for Ms. Adams, yet you will not allow me the same courtesy for my own daughter?"

"That was different. From what you're telling me now, Ms. Adams is being accused of assaulting the wee lassie. I hardly think you being present at her interrogation will help matters, do you?"

"And our being at Samach house will?"

"It's not ideal. Personally, I'd recommend you find alternative accommodation for the duration. It's be easier to reach you with news if you were in the city."

Midnight considered this. What Anderson said made sense but something told him that he needed to be nearer to

Glenhaven than Edinburgh, if only to keep an eye on his cousin and her alleged change in behaviour.

Anderson continued, "However, if you insist on staying at the cottage, I cannae stop you."

"Will you allow Inspector Gredge to accompany you to Glenhaven?"

"I suppose so. If it'll keep you out of the way."

"I'll be there. Every step of the way until the girl is found," Gredge declared in an unarguable tone.

"I can assure you all," Anderson said, eyeing each of them in turn, "that I will do everything in my power to recover your loved one." Tense silence hung in the air as did the unspoken but inferred words 'dead or alive'. Anderson cleared his throat. "I'll send for a cab to take us to the coach station. I'll drop you off at Samach and continue on to Glenhaven with Inspector Gredge. No doubt he'll fill you in when he returns. In the meantime, Lord Gunn, I would encourage you to stay away from Ms. Adams and let us do our job."

THE COACH TRIP had been no less uncomfortable than Anderson's office. Their only respite from the bumps and jostles being the remnants of Mrs. P.'s pigeon pie that she'd hastily shoved into a hamper before they'd left London. Midnight had declined his portion for fear the pie had gone off after hours on a stuffy train and an equally stuffy office. Besides, he had little appetite as things stood. His worry for Polly overriding any hunger. Anderson had told him to steer clear of his cousin, but not of her staff, and there was still Charlie and Laura, whom he was sure would relate the events as accurately, if not more so, than the Glenhaven staff.

When they pulled up outside Samach Cottage, it was late and the building looked cold and empty. No lights shone in the windows and no one came out to greet them. He was surprised to admit that he felt more than a little deflated. Mrs. P. would soon have the stove lit and the place feeling homely, but it wouldn't be the same without Polly and the others. He usually craved solitude, but this time he felt the need to have his people near.

"Arthur, when you're done up at the house, would you mind instructing my staff to return to the cottage as soon as they can? I take it I am allowed my own staff back, Inspector?" He directed this last part at Anderson who shrugged.

"After I've interviewed them, aye. Did you not say you'd left them at Glenhaven to take care of Ms. Adams though?"

"I did, but by the sound of things, Ms. Adams is in no need of their assistance anymore with the exception of Charlie perhaps. I should still like them here nonetheless. Arthur?"

"Yeah, I'll escort them back myself. How many bedrooms did you say this place has?" Gredge asked, eyeing up the cottage.

"Six," Midnight replied.

"Hmm." Gredge grunted, mentally tallying up how many people would soon be sleeping under its roof.

"We'll figure something out. I need them here, Arthur."

"Righto." Gredge handed Giles his small suitcase, tipped his bowler and reached forward to close the carriage door.

Anderson leaned towards the window. "I'll be returning to the city in the coach when I'm done, but I'll send word if I have any news. I'm sure the good Inspector here will fill you in on events up at the house. I've got a team out looking for the dog as we speak, the best trackers I could find. I'm sure it won't be long before we get a lead, Lord Gunn."

Midnight banged the carriage door twice and the driver clicked his reins. As the coach moved forward, Midnight replied, "I trust it won't, Inspector. I am relying on you." The words were spoken to Anderson but it was Gredge who acknowledged him with the slightest nod.

THE WAIT WAS AGONISING. After the second hour had passed, and he had checked his pocket watch for the hundredth time, Midnight could not stomach being inside any longer.

"I'm taking a walk to the stables," he announced to the occupants of the kitchen.

Giles Morgan rose. "Very well, sir. I shall fetch your coat."

"And your own if you feel like some fresh air?" Midnight offered.

Giles nodded.

"Mrs. P., there will be seven of us for dinner this evening. Have we enough food in the pantry to cover it?"

"There's enough to be going on with. Plenty of eggs from the hens and some cold meats. I'm sure I can rustle up something."

"I've no doubt. If Inspector Gredge comes back in the meantime, would you kindly send him to the stables? I want to talk with him as soon as he's back."

"Right away, sir."

Midnight nodded his thanks, and he and Giles set off at a brisk pace towards the stable yard.

"I would've thought Charlie might've come to the

cottage by now. He must know that we're here," Midnight said.

"It is probable that the inspectors have them all up at the house being interviewed one by one. It may be that they won't allow anyone to leave until they're done," Giles replied.

"You're right, of course. I just couldn't sit in that parlour any longer. I feel so useless. I need to be doing something. I need to be out searching for my daughter."

"Best we know where to begin first. As soon as Inspector Gredge returns we'll have more to go on."

Midnight glanced sideways at his old butler. He was no spring chicken, but he was still quite fit for a man of his age and just as stalwart as ever. There was no question that Giles had included himself in the proposed search party. Polly was loved by all of the Gunn household, and the more people included in the search, the better. All he needed was a starting point from which to begin. *Blast it!* If Anderson had only allowed him to be a part of the interrogation process, he was sure he would've been out looking by now. Every second that ticked by was a second too long. If he could just find Charlie at the stables, he might be able to glean enough information to form the beginnings of a plan of action or at least feel like he was actually doing something proactive.

They never made it to the stables, for just ahead, down the road that led to the main house, were Gredge, Charlie and Agnes, hurrying towards him at a fair pace. The looks on their faces told him everything he needed to know and he felt his stomach turn with sickening dread.

21

A LESSON IN LOVE

"**B**lowing your top ain't going to help either of those girls, Midnight."

"She should be in custody! None of this makes any sense whatsoever. Lau—Miss Carter would not poison anyone, and as for Wick and Craigson, well, of course they're going to back up whatever concocted bullhog their mistress has cooked up."

"Look, you above all people know how these things work. It's your man Charlie's and Miss Carmichael's word against theirs, and seeing as neither of them were present at this attempted poisoning, the butler and cook are the only witnesses."

"But they *all* saw that... that *woman* strike my daughter!"

"True enough, but again, their stories don't match those of Master Fenwick or Miss Carmichael. All we have are the facts as told to us. What's important now is deciding what we can do to find Polly and your maid. Now, Charlie knows that Miss Carter followed the wolf thing into the forest to the west of the house, and we know there's a range of hills surrounding the property. My guess is it has a den somewhere in those hills to the west. I'd suggest the four of us—"

"Five," piped up Mrs. P.

"Six, if you please," Agnes chimed in, folding her arms in defiance.

"Ladies, as much as I appreciate it—"

"We have legs, Inspector. If you're about to suggest that we cannot participate in the search due to our gender, then I—"

"Can we all just stop?" Midnight shouted above the commotion.

Five pairs of eyes turned in his direction.

"Please. This is getting us nowhere. Quite frankly, I don't give a flying fig who comes along, just as long as we get going." He turned to Clementine. "Dearest Mrs. P., as much as I'd be glad to have you along, I do need someone to stay here just in case Polly or Miss Carter come back. They will need attending to if they do and you're the one to do it. Nobody nurtures like you." He smiled kindly at her, and she conceded with a brief nod. "Miss Carmichael, you may of course accompany us if you're feeling well enough. Not to sound harsh, but another body to care for is not what I need should your cold return with a vengeance."

"I am fit enough, Lord Gunn. If I feel unwell at any point, I promise to return to the cottage at once. Besides, I cannot sit here and wait I... I feel somewhat... responsible for, oh!" Agnes's face crumpled in anguish. "It's my fault! I should've done something." Giles handed her his handkerchief, which she took and blew her nose loudly.

Midnight let out a sigh. Tensions were running high. Everyone was worried about the two missing members of their little family.

"You mustn't think that, Miss Carmichael. It is not the

fault of anyone in this room. There are larger things at play here, but we must all work together now and find our girls. So, I propose Inspector Gredge take Giles and Miss Carmichael and work to the east of the house. Charlie and I will take the west. Look for the deer trails. It's likely that the beast will follow those routes through the forest. Keep an eye on the ground for footprints, dung, anything that would indicate which direction it might have taken. Once you reach the summit of the hill, spread out upon the descent but stay within range of each other. That way we can cover more ground yet still be close enough to help if one of us should need it. Are we agreed?"

They all nodded. Agnes gulped looking a tad pale but also nodded. Gredge, Giles, and Midnight checked their pistols and ammunition, Agnes gripped the iron fire poker from the hearth so tightly it sent her knuckles white, and Charlie brandished his pitchfork from the stables with such determination he would've put a Templar Knight to shame.

"Let's be off then," Gredge instructed. "See you at the summit."

Their ascent on the western hill was long and laborious despite their following clear paths through the brush. The ground was soggy and slippery underfoot, and it didn't take long before both Midnight and Charlie had slid on their backsides more than once. Neither man complained. However, their focus was entirely fixed on tracking the beast and the two girls. After an hour's huffing and puffing, traversing burns and clambering over fallen trees, they stopped to catch their breath and check their direction.

Charlie plonked himself down on a boulder, took off his right shoe, and groaned. "Whoar! I got bleedin' blisters already. 'Ow far do you reckon we are from the top, sir?"

"Another hour should do it. Let me see your foot."

Midnight crouched over Charlie's elevated leg and turned the foot to examine the damage. "That's a nasty one. Let me heal that for you. You don't want it to get infected."

Charlie grimaced at the thought and gave his consent. Blisters were an easy fix for Midnight. The raw pustules were nothing but faded pink blotches within seconds, causing Charlie to heave a sigh of relief.

"You'd've made a cracking doctor, you know," Charlie declared most sincerely as he began to lace up his boot.

"I considered it—once, before my father died. He was not convinced on the idea, thought I'd stand out too much and someone would discover what I really was. He was afraid I'd be imprisoned in an institution and studied like an animal in a cage. We compromised in the end. I agreed to not study medicine, and in turn, he let me visit the poorer parts of the city to do what I could for the people of London in relative secrecy. It worked quite well for a while."

They continued their ascent as they conversed.

"Beggin' your pardon, your lordship, but... might I ask, what *are* you exactly?" Charlie asked a little sheepishly.

Midnight didn't mind the question. Indeed, he'd expected it would pop up in conversation at some point seeing as he'd been the one to save Charlie's and Laura's souls from that blackguard, Nightingale. He wrinkled his brow. "Do you know, Charlie, I have been asking myself that very question for years? In truth, I really don't know what I am. My father and I have read countless books on the occult, ancient mythology, even various religious texts in the hope of finding an answer. I confess I'm no nearer to discovering one than I was a decade ago. It used to play heavily on my mind until Giles found me in my study one night, asleep on a pile of books."

"What did he do?" said Charlie intrigued.

"Sent me to bed with a few wise words," Midnight replied, smiling. "I remember it like it was yesterday. He said, 'A person's life should meaningful. *What* you are is far less important than *who* you are. Perhaps you should focus on that first. Knowing who you are will determine what you become.' And so, I gave up searching for a label and set about discovering who I am and what sort of person I want to be. I confess I'm still finding that out." He chuckled.

Charlie grinned. "Makes a lot of sense, does old Morgan. I'll remember that. *Who* is Charlie Fenwick? Make it me own mission to find out, I will."

"You're a good man, Charlie."

"So are you, sir."

A respectful silence fell between them until Charlie piped up suddenly. "Laura finks you're an angel."

Midnight stubbed his toe on a tree root and cursed.

Charlie sniggered behind his hand. "Reckons you're a gift from God, she does."

"Hardly," Midnight mumbled, not liking the direction the conversation was going. "Here. Let's go this way. I see a rock formation up ahead," he said in an attempt to change the subject.

"We've talked about it—you, I mean—a lot since... well, you know, since we came to work for you. 'Ope you don't mind me saying, sir?"

"I can hardly censor your private conversations, now can I?" Midnight replied, struggling to disguise the discouraging tone in his voice. The thought of his housemaid musing over his origins with Charlie filled him with horror. He was tempted to demand what sort of claptrap they'd come up with between them but his manners wouldn't allow it. Besides, he wasn't naive enough to think they wouldn't have talked about him in private. He had just admitted to himself that he'd expected one or both of them to ask at some point. So why was he on the defensive now?

"Nah, I suppose not," said Charlie, completely oblivious to his master's discomfort. "Well, it don't matter really, does it? I mean it's like you said, init? You're a good soul, regardless. And me and Laura's ever so grateful to ya." Charlie blew out a long breath. "I 'ope we find 'em soon."

"As do I," Midnight said, grateful for the change in conversation.

"If I know the little miss and our Laura, they'll be givin' it 'ell anyway, eh?"

Midnight turned his head to offer Charlie a conciliatory smile even though his gut had just turned a somersault. He glanced skywards at the rolling clouds and peeking sunbeams. There were only a few hours of daylight left.

If I am an angel, pray that I find my charges before the light fails me. Whether it was the fading daylight or his own light that he thought of, he wasn't sure.

"There!" Charlie cried. Pushing past Midnight, he fell to his knees scrabbling for something on the ground. He turned and held up his find.

"A stocking."

"Laura's, I reckon," Charlie said. Midnight barely resisted the urge to enquire as to just how Charlie knew it to be an item of Miss Carter's undergarments when—

"Gotta be; it's got blood on it look. That's where that dog bit her."

Midnight took the stocking and stuffed it in his pocket, uncomfortable with it being on display despite there being no one around, save Charlie, to see it.

"At least we're on the right track."

"Shall we signal the others, you reckon, sir?"

"I think it's best. We might need back-up." Midnight

withdrew his pistol from its holster and fired a single shot into the air. "That should do it. Gredge will find us. Let's continue up this trail. It'll be getting dark soon."

They reached the rocky outcrop that Midnight had spotted earlier. Partially hidden by trees was a small cave just large enough for an average sized person to crawl into for shelter. A brief inspection turned up no evidence of either Polly or Laura having used it, but there were a few scattered animal bones hidden amongst the leaf matter near the entrance.

"What you finkin'? Is it its den?" Charlie asked.

"Something has used it as a stopover from time to time, but the cave is too small to offer anything other than temporary shelter. And there's this." Midnight reached forward to pluck some fur from a nearby bush. "It's coarse. Doesn't seem like anything I've seen before."

Charlie used the prongs of his pitchfork to disperse more of the leaf litter surrounding the entrance but found nothing. "Onwards an' upwards then, eh?"

"Indeed." With each step Midnight's heart constricted a little more. He was relieved to have found only animal bones in the den-- anything human didn't bear thinking about. A few hundred yards up the trail their luck changed for the better.

"Bleedin' 'ell, they're huge!" Cried Charlie, referring to the set of disconcertingly large paw prints they'd discovered.

"Mmm." Midnight agreed. Having seen the beast first hand, he could attest to its stature. "Proof we are definitely on the right track at least. I'm no expert but these look fairly fresh. Best we stay alert now, Charlie."

"Aye. Can you feel anyfink?" Midnight took a moment to focus, then shook his head.

"Nothing yet. I'll let you know if I do. Eyes and ears

open." He indicated up the trail. The trees thinned out nearer the summit. He hoped they might garner a better view of their surroundings from there. He stood for a moment, staring ahead and chewing his lip.

"We'll find 'em, sir. I know it."

"Thank you, Charlie." That was all he could manage to say. He didn't want to give voice to the deep-seated fear of what would happen if they didn't find them, or worse, if they did but they were— He shook the thought from his mind.

Back at the cottage, when Charlie had described in horrifying detail how the beast had held his daughter in its jaws and carried her off, it had taken every ounce of self-control he had to keep from charging into Glenhaven and blasting the whole place to Hell. He'd left his daughter in the care of that woman and now she was gone, perhaps forever. And poor Miss Carter too. After everything she'd been through already, to now be injured and missing because she'd been protecting his daughter, when it should've been him. He should have been here to protect them all.

His trip to London had been a conspiracy to lure him away from Polly. He was convinced that somehow that villainous bastard, Hemlock Nightingale, was behind it all and was in league with this rabid Barghest as well as those pesky Pookas. Well, this time there would be no getting away. He would end Nightingale for good and any creature that followed him. But first he had to find them.

He puzzled over how Nightingale had managed to enlist the help of four Fae. They were unlikely to collaborate with the half-breed monstrosity that he had been the night when Midnight pushed him off Westminster Bridge, had he managed to rid himself of that cursed body? Had he offered the Fae a treasure so tempting that they couldn't resist? The Pooka had wanted his land, but the Barghest? What could Nightingale possibly offer that beast? And then the answer came to him in a flash.

"Polly!"

"Where?" cried Charlie.

"No. The Barghest—it took Polly as payment for helping Hemlock. I'm sure of it."

"But why? What would a wolf want with a girl?"

"Polly has powers; the beast is fae. It probably wants to use her or—Jesus Christ—*feed* on her to increase its own power. I don't know why exactly but I'm sure I'm right. And what's more," he said as they reached the top of the hill giving them an unrestricted view into the distance, "I know where it is."

22

THE STONES

They didn't have to wait long for Gredge, Giles, and Agnes to catch up to them. They met them on the descent. Gredge had been quick to respond to his signal, and he and Midnight spoke in hurried tones as their whole party raced back down the hill as fast as they were able in the dimming light.

"There's no time to fetch Anderson. Charlie, I need you to saddle two horses—"

"Three!" Giles huffed.

"Fine. Three horses." He had no time to argue. Giles had suffered on the long train journey north, but Midnight knew protestation was futile. The old butler would either accompany them or die trying. He loved Polly as much as any of them, and Midnight had to admit that Giles was pretty handy with a pistol. Having Gredge and Giles as back-up was more than most men could ask for.

"Aye, sir," Charlie said.

"Then I need you to keep an eye on Glenhaven. Make a note of anyone coming or going, but keep out of sight."

"Done."

"Miss Carmichael, go straight back to the cottage and help Mrs. Philips prepare whatever she needs. There might be injuries to tend to when we return. Whatever you do, keep the doors locked. Your father would never forgive me if anything should happen to you."

"Yes, sir. Understood."

Midnight was glad that nobody felt the need to contradict his instructions. He knew he could rely on each of them to do as he asked, Gredge and Giles most of all. The Inspector even seemed eager to get on with the plan. It was amusing to see just how much Polly had gotten under everyone's skins. Unless... it was Miss Carter that Gredge was so keen to find? Arthur was single, after all, and eligible, and he could offer her a decent home. A rush of heated emotion flooded Midnight's chest. But *he* could offer her more than if she were the wife of a policeman, a better home a—

Oh stop it you fool! What nonsense. She doesn't even want you, and even if she did, it could never happen. The realisation that he might, in fact, have feelings for his housemaid struck him as utterly ridiculous even as his fingers remembered the feel of her hand in his. *You should be shot, you deplorable cad! Lords do not marry their maids.*

Their descent took half the time that their ascent had. Thankfully, they'd all made it to the stable yard without anyone buckling an ankle on the steep, darkening trail. Midnight escorted Agnes back to within sight of Samach Cottage and watched her enter the small front garden before hastening back to where Charlie was saddling Gorgon and Samson. Arthur Gredge looked decidedly green.

"You have ridden before, Arthur?" Midnight asked.

"Not exactly, no," Arthur replied, tugging his moustache. "Can't be that hard, can it?"

"You're about to find out. Just grip with your knees and steer with the reins, and try not to fall off."

"Right."

Giles emerged from the stables, leading the Spanish Jennet that belonged to Ms. Adams, a saddle in his hands. "This one seems calm, perhaps the Inspector would prefer to ride her?"

Arthur eyed Gorgon and the Jennet, Birdie. The mare was smaller and did appear to have a gentle manner.

"Less distance to fall, I suppose," Arthur surmised and opted for the Jennet. He took the reins from Giles while the butler saddled the horse for him.

"All done, sir." Charlie said. "I'll be off to keep an eye out now then."

"Good man, Charlie. Remember to stay out of sight and be careful. Any sign of trouble, head for the cottage and protect the women," Midnight instructed, hauling himself up on to Samson's back once more.

"Gotcha. You be careful, 'n'all, eh?" Charlie said, looking at each man in turn. "Bring 'em 'ome."

"How the blazes do I actually get on this bloody thing?"

Everyone looked at Gredge who was staring at the stirrup like it was a foreign object.

Charlie smiled and offered him a leg up which Gredge gratefully accepted. "Try to relax, Inspector. Just move with the 'orse. She'll see you right."

"If you say so." He looked decidedly doubtful.

Charlie gave the horse a gentle slap on the rump and watched the three men ride away, two of them gracefully competent, the other hanging on for dear life.

Midnight tried not to let his frustration with Gredge show. Giles was an excellent horseman and had no trouble keeping pace with him. Gredge was a different matter; he bounced along, trying to hang on as best he could, almost toppling from his saddle a few times. A copious amount of curse words flew from the inspector's mouth, which had the situation been different, Midnight would've found highly amusing. Their way was marred even further by the ever-dimming daylight, which made it harder to see the road ahead. He pushed on knowing that they must reach the castle *and* make it up the hill before full dark.

"Are you sure this is the right way?" Gredge called from behind. "You said you'd only visited it once."

"Just try to keep up," Midnight yelled back.

The wind was getting up, and he was thankful that it wasn't currently raining. It took the best part of an hour, riding at full pelt, to reach the dilapidated gates of the ruined castle of *Cnoc Sithe*, the place he had visited with Polly, the place they'd chosen as their future summer home. *Pray that she has a future.* His guts twisted at that injurious thought.

This was the second time the girl had been taken from him and put in harm's way. So far, he wasn't impressed by his ability to protect her. Was this what being a parent was going to be like, living in constant fear for your child's wellbeing?

The party of three tied their horses to nearby trees and squeezed past the rusted iron. Midnight's heart was hammering in his chest. He was trying to hurry, but the bumpy, overgrown path proved difficult to navigate. He felt the familiar thrum of magic as its energy pulled him closer to his goal. Upon his last visit, he'd been convinced the energies surrounding this place were benign, even welcoming, so it made no sense that such a malicious beast should take refuge nearby. As they entered the building, he heard the exclamations of his two companions, but their mutterings merely washed over him. His focus was entirely on getting to what lay beyond the castle atop the tree-covered hill, the place from whence the power came. Barreling through the rear door, he stood once more to look upon the source of the magical energy. The view was the same as the last time, only now he knew what awaited at the summit.

"I don't see the stones, sir." Giles panted.

"You can't from this side. The trees are blocking them, and we're much lower down than from where we saw them before. They're there."

"Best get a move on, then. It'll be dark when we reach the top," Arthur said.

"You both need to be careful. We're about to encounter the unknown, even to me, and I can't be distracted, which means I need you both to look out for each other."

"And you, sir," Giles stated.

"Don't give me a second thought." He paused for a moment. "If anything should happen to me—"

Gredge placed a reassuring hand on Midnight's shoulder. "We'll find them."

"You can count on us, sir."

"Yes. Yes I can." Midnight acknowledged them both with a brief nod.

For so many years he had felt it necessary to keep himself hidden, and Giles had always been his constant. Then he'd met Gredge, who had proved himself a trustworthy colleague and loyal friend time and again. He could not think of two better people to have by his side when facing whatever lay ahead.

Less steep than their previous climb had been, the men clambered uphill without hindrance or hesitation. The ground was soft but not soggy, and there was a distinct pathway weaving through the trees and undergrowth, indi-

cating it was used regularly by wildlife or men. As they journeyed on, Midnight focused on the image he'd seen of this
place from the viewpoint of the larger hill they'd climbed
earlier. The moment his eyes had fallen upon the stone
circle, he'd known that this ring of ancient jagged sentries
was where he needed to be. It lay in the same direction
Charlie had said the Barghest had headed with Polly. It was
brimming with magical energy, and if memory served, he
remembered reading theories regarding stone circles and
how they might act as portals to the 'otherworld'. He'd
already had the encounter with the three Pooka, and Bobby
Mac had been certain the Barghest was a creature of the
Fae, they must be coming from somewhere. Scotland was
known for its fairy hills. Indeed, Mr. Gavill himself had
informed him that the very house he intended to buy was
named so in Gaelic. It all seemed too much of a coincidence
to not be connected. He did not know if he would find Polly
and Miss Carter nearby but he was sure he would find that
confounded beast that had taken his daughter and attacked
his housemaid. And when he found it, he would make it
pay. The Barghest *and* Hemlock-bloody-Nightingale.

"I don't like this place," Gredge said, the unease in his
voice clear. "It gives me the willies." He had his pistol ready
and cocked and had adopted a sort of hunter's stance as if
he were deer stalking, expecting something nasty to jump
out and attack suddenly. Giles also looked uneasy.
Midnight's gun was still in its hip holster. He was preparing
to draw on his own powers if needed.

The great megalithic monument before him struck him
as decidedly different to any he'd seen before. It wasn't just
the way they were positioned, which was unlike any he'd
seen illustrated in his books, but the very feel of the place.
He had of course visited the infamous Stonehenge in Salis-

bury many years ago with his father, Josiah Gunn, and the great rings at Avebury in Wiltshire. Both sites bloomed with what he would call 'natural' energy. This place felt different, neither natural or unnatural, if that made any sense.

"Wait here. Stay alert. I need to walk the stones," Midnight instructed his companions.

"What's he mean, *walk the stones?*" Gredge whispered to Giles, who just shrugged.

Midnight stepped through the gap in the two stones that faced each other. As he did so he felt a sickening twist deep in his gut. The sensation put him so off kilter that he came close to losing the contents of his stomach.

"Sir?" Giles called, ready to step to his master's aid.

Midnight held up a hand to indicate his was all right and staggered towards the centre of the circle. The only source of light available to him now was the moon, swollen with ethereal radiance. Focusing on its celestial glow, he drank in the power of Selene, the ancient Greek moon goddess. Moonlight healed him well enough but always left him cold, unlike the warmth of the sun's rays or that of flames which revived him faster and were easier to access. As he opened his mind and allowed the gossamer light into his body, the wave of dizziness dissipated. Once more steady on his feet, he continued forward to touch the outer most stone. Cold and hard to the touch, the dark basalt felt paradoxically alive under his hand. Tiny pinpricks of energy tickled his open palm, probing, investigating. He walked on, touching each stone in turn, his anticipation and curiosity building, until he came back to the two giants that guarded the circle's entrance. These made him nervous. Dare he touch them? Stepping closer, Midnight reached out an explorative hand. His fingers were inches away when he felt a great force pushing him away, it was as if the stones them-selves were repellent.

"Interesting," he muttered.

He tried again, only to have the same thing happen. Steeling himself, he inhaled the sweet night air of the Pent-land Hills and called the shadows to him. A thousand needles penetrated his skin as he soaked up the swirling darkness, bringing the power of the shadows inside him. He opened his hands and sent a plume of roiling smoke from his palms towards the space between the stones. The ground beneath his feet shook in protest as the smoke hit an unseen barrier at the centre of the gap. Sweating, he pushed harder, all the while using spirals of dark power to probe for any week spots or openings, but the stones pushed back, eventually beating him.

Midnight let go of the shadows with huge effort, once again turning his gaze towards the night sky now sprinkled with stars. The light of Selene shone down on him. Free of the dark, he opened himself to the light and sent forth a wave of twisting tendrils towards the towering monoliths. This time the air around him vibrated with a low frequency hum, and instead of repelling him, he found himself being pulled forward towards the gap which had now begun to glow blue. He channeled more light into it. The glow increased, as did the noise and vibration. He was captivated by it and barely heard the urgent shouts of his companions over the enchanting noise. Nor did he hear the piercing boom that ricocheted around the clearing. The space opened into a wide vortex of swirling blue light, so allur-ingly bright it became almost blinding but he could not look away, no matter how hard he tried. There were shapes at its centre and they were moving. Something was coming towards him.

Another loud bang rang out into the night. The hairs on the back of his neck prickled. That was his only warning as a pain like nothing he'd ever felt before tore through his left arm.

He fell, momentarily confused. Warm liquid ran down his wrist, he smelled the coppery scent of blood. The power had left him the instant the bullet had entered his body, but the portal remained open and positively buzzed with energy.

"I've been shot," he stated in a somewhat detached tone. The fog of enchantment wore off quite suddenly when the realisation of his injury hit him. "I've been shot!"

He looked in the direction of where he knew Gredge and Giles to be but could see nothing save the glaring light that threatened to seduce him once more. He squinted against it and turned his face skyward. He needed to heal himself fast. The shapes in the portal were approaching at frightening speed. He must have full use of his arm in readiness to face whatever entity was about to fall upon him. The moonlight paled in comparison to the gleaming magnificence of that other realm but he held fast just enough to draw on the healing light to staunch the bleeding. The magnetic pull of the portal increased as a shadowy form began to burst through the thin veil that separated the world of men from the world of the Fae. Midnight craned his neck, desperate to see beyond the shadowy hulk into the magical world beyond.

The lines of a recently published poem entitled 'Goblin Market' by a Miss Christina Rossetti came suddenly to mind.

> 'Laura stretched her gleaming neck
> Like a rush-imbedded swan,

Like a lily from the beck,
Like a moonlit poplar branch,
Like a vessel at the launch
When its last restraint is gone.
Backwards up the mossy glen
Turned and trooped the goblin men,
With their shrill repeated cry,
'Come buy, come buy.'

Just like the girl in the poem, he was mesmerised, thrilled by the sheer magisterial mystical power that radiated from beyond. In that briefest of moments nothing else existed except him and the overwhelming temptation to escape through that open door to a world of untold wonder. The noises surrounding him, the panicked cries of his companions, the damp grass upon which he sat all faded from view as he began to drift, to allow himself to be sucked into that blissful otherworldly abyss.

23

REALITY BITES

"Get up, man! Midnight!"

He heard his name and recognised, but didn't understand, the urgency in the caller's shout. He didn't want to get up. He was peaceful and carefree for the first time in his life.

"For the love of God, get up! Help us!"

Midnight sighed. His fingers toyed with the dewy blades of grass upon which he sat without worry. His brow furrowed. The intrusion annoyed him a little, and then he heard a word that wrenched him from his enchanted state causing reality to strike with all the force of a sudden rockfall.

"Hemlock!"

In a rush of noise, realisation sparked into focus kick-starting him into action. Midnight scrambled to his feet, drawing in as much of the shadows and the moonlight together as he could safely contain and pelted towards Gredge whom he now knew to be the one who had shouted. The scene that greeted him was one of startling chaos.

Giles was wrestling a vaguely familiar man dressed in a

black suit who had extensive scarring around his face and neck—*Mr. Rosemont?*—and a woman, whose back was turned but he immediately recognised as Ms. Adams, was beating the butler with a riding crop. Gredge meanwhile was struggling, pinned to the floor whilst that bastard, Hemlock Nightingale, rained down blow after blow upon his already swollen face. He had seconds to decide. Gredge could handle himself in most situations, but Midnight knew from personal experience just how strong Hemlock was. But Giles was fighting off two attackers who, by all intents and purposes, were hellbent on killing the older man. He couldn't choose between them, and yet he could not let the chance to kill that demon-spawn escape him again.

He ran towards Gredge, firing a fusion of light and dark power in passing at the man who was now trying to strangle his butler. From the corner of his eye, he saw the man crumple and fall. Ms. Adams renewed her attack with vigour, and Midnight had no time to ponder on the whys and wherefores of either his cousin's presence or the reason for her bewildering behavior, but he quickly surmised that Giles would put aside his 'correct conduct hat' in this instance and somehow manage to subdue the woman.

He was almost upon the Hemlock-Gredge heap of flying fists when he noticed more bodies emerging from the trees. The thought *Who are these people and why are they attacking?* barely entered his mind when Hemlock, who had beaten Gredge into a state of semi-consciousness, noticed Midnight's approach and pounced, knocking him to the ground.

Midnight landed hard on his back, and he felt all of the air leaving his body in one big painful *whomp*. Hemlock was on top of him in an instant, his hands wrapped around Midnight's throat, squeezing with all of his might. A bizarre sense of déja vu settled over him. He might've seen the irony in it if not for the stinging of tears that rolled from the corners of his eyes which, he was sure, were now bulging from their sockets, about to pop. Still winded, his natural instinct was to fight for breath. His mouth made the motions, but no air could enter his lungs. Tiny black spots marred his vision, and the ringing in his ears grew louder. He was dying. This bastard was going to beat him.

"I'm going to enjoy watching the light leave your eyes, Gunn," Hemlock hissed. "And then I'm going to devour everything that you own. You took everything from me, and now I'm taking it all back," he spat.

Even through his impaired vision, Midnight could tell that Nightingale was no longer the deformed, monstrous creature that he'd encountered on Westminster Bridge all those months ago—wild-eyed and murderous, yes, but beastly and demonic no, at least not outwardly. His human form belied a strength of inhuman proportions.

Hemlock squeezed harder. Midnight could hardly make out the face above him now. He clawed frantically at the man on top of him, trying to gain purchase, trying to remember how he called on his powers. He had a vague recollection of having a gun somewhere about his person but couldn't quite process the thought with any conviction.

"How does it feel, swine, to know you will die and I will live on? Retribution is mine! I am unstoppable now. I have ensured my victory and my vengeance will be eternal. Your soul is mine!"

No! It couldn't end like this. This was not how it was supposed to work. From the recesses of his mind he heard a scream.

"Papa!"

The hands around his neck loosened ever so slightly but

it was enough. He'd heard his daughter's cry and knew she was *alive*. That was all the motivation he needed. There was no chance in Hell he would allow Polly to witness his demise at the hands of the pig who had once tried to claim her life for himself. And he knew that if Hemlock succeeded in killing him, his next target would be Polly. With every ounce of power still left in him, and with formidable effort, Midnight threw everything he had at his enemy.

Hemlock growled and renewed his efforts but was sent reeling backwards. He flew through the air and smashed into one of the standing stones where he tumbled to the ground in a heap.

Midnight forced a reviving breath down into his lungs. His throat burned, but he exhaled, pushing past the pain to again draw in air, in and out, until his vision returned and he didn't have to tell his body to breathe.

The heap rolled over and used the stone to claw his way back to a standing position, Hemlock snarled in his direction and prepared to charge.

Midnight wondered how Hemlock had recovered so quickly. Was the man indeed still possessed by the demonic soul he'd used to perform his previous dastardly deeds? Midnight's brow furrowed; Hemlock's incensed expression was wild but entirely human- not a hint of the horribly mutated features that had once graced that snaring visage. Then where had the man found such strength and resilience?

"Papa!"

The cry of his daughter filled him with such fear for her safety that he wanted to shout at her to run away but at the same time he had the desperate need to run to her and protect her from Hemlock's imminent attack. Concentrating hard, Midnight launched another stream of dark power as Hemlock advanced on him at speed. The blow struck him square in the chest and again sent him barreling through the air where Midnight heard a satisfying crack as Hemlock's skull struck stone and the bastard finally lay still.

Midnight scanned the darkness for his daughter and saw her running towards him, arms spread wide and ready for his embrace. A quick glance to where Hemlock lay, still unmoving, reassured him that she was in no immediate danger and yet— He snapped his eyes back to Polly. A great dark shape came lumbering after her, its slavering snarling jaws gnashing, eyes on its target, and the bottom dropped out of his stomach.

Midnight opened his hand, ready to strike but she was in the way. "Polly, move!" The words came out in a barely audible croak. Luckily, Polly saw the fear in his expression as she drew near him, and the direction of his stare.

She stopped and looked behind her and then did the strangest thing. "Papa, stop! Don't hurt him!" She'd ceased running and stood between him and the shaggy beast, her arms outstretched in a protective manner.

Confusion stayed his hand. What was she doing? He had his answer when the Barghest, unwavering from its directive, veered to the right to avoid colliding with the girl. It continued straight towards Midnight and jumped. If it hadn't had been for Polly's insistent cry of 'let him pass', he would've struck the creature mid-leap. And leap it did, straight over him, landing directly in front of the inert form of Nightingale.

Polly fell into his arms. He buried his face in the mass of sweet-smelling curls and breathed her in. "Polly," he croaked, "you're alive. Oh, thank God. You're alive."

"Well, course I am." She sobbed happily into his neck.

"But, how? That creature, it took you away and Charlie said—"

"His name is Widdershins, and he *saved* me, Papa." Polly lifted her head and looked to where the Barghest was advancing menacingly on the crumpled form of Hemlock Nightingale who had again begun to stir.

Midnight scrambled to his feet, shoving the girl behind him. He looked around for Gredge and Giles so that he might send her to them, but they were occupied in a fight of their own. Gredge, having recovered from his severe beating, was on his feet again shouting instructions to Giles and... *Laura!* What in Bathsheba's backside was she doing here? This evening was turning out to be one of shock and surprise to say the very least. He could see that the two men and his maid were standing a few feet apart in a line formation with Gredge at the centre. The Inspector was wielding a gun and shooting at the ground. Giles and Laura were kicking and stamping for all they were worth. What on Earth were they doing?

His eyes widened in alarm when a tattered arm rose from the ground near where Laura stood. The hand on the end of the arm made a grab for her ankle, and she screeched, jumping back. Gredge aimed and fired and the raggedy limb fell limply onto the damp earth.

They're killing people! And it was a lot of people too by the looks of things.

Midnight stood in the middle of the mayhem and for the first time in a long time, he didn't know what to do. Hemlock wasn't yet dead, his friends were seemingly on a killing spree, and he had no safe place in which to hide Polly. Protecting her was his only option. Hemlock would have to wait, and so would Gredge and the others. He would deal with whatever was happening there later. He needed to get his daughter to safety and if that meant abandoning this hilltop and everyone on it, then so be it. Taking the girl's hand, he said, "We need to go. Now." He turned to leave, but she tugged him back.

"No, Papa. They need your help." She implored him, her gaze turned towards her beloved Laura, Giles and Gredge. He followed her gaze and frowned, still not understanding. "They're linked to 'im, all the missing dead people. He's controlling them. 'Shins told me."

"Dead people?"

"Ugh!" Polly stamped her foot in frustration. "Ms. Adams, the lot of them!" She pointed her stump to the heap of bodies that were crawling and clambering on the ground, still trying to grasp for Gredge and his army of two. The penny dropped. Midnight looked from the small tribe of writhing bodies to the rising form of his enemy who was focused on the snarling beast that barred his escape. Somehow, Hemlock had forged himself a legion of the living dead, his cousin included, he now realised with horror. How, he did not yet understand, but if he survived this night, he would make it his mission to find out. Right now, his only concern was protecting those he loved.

"Shins is... that thing?" He indicated to the Barghest which was advancing most menacingly on Hemlock.

"Yes!"

"And *he* is your—"

"My friend! Now go, help them!" She stamped her foot again.

"Stay right there, and don't move."

"Go!" Polly squealed.

Midnight hurried over to Gredge.

"About bloody time! Where's your weapon?" Gredge yelled. Midnight's hand flew to his hip, relief flooded him as his fingers touched hard, cold steel. "Now shoot the buggers!"

"Who are they?" Midnight shouted back.

"Who cares? They ain't out for a shitting Sunday stroll. Some of 'em look like they just crawled out of the grave. Shoot, man!" *BANG!* Gredge let off another round, hitting the animated corpse of an unknown man with half of his face rotted away.

"Jesus Christ." The scene was too much to believe, even for Midnight. Dead people, alive again? One of them half-rose from the ground and scuttled towards him. He fired on impulse, and its head exploded spattering decomposing brain matter and bone. He fought off repulsion and took aim again. "Laura," he shouted, "go to Polly."

He looked at her, and she looked at him. Something unspoken passed between them, and she gave him the briefest of smiles, picked up her skirts and hobbled towards her charge.

"Morgan, to your left!" Gredge yelled. Giles sprang aside and launched a well-aimed boot at the nearby skeletal form that had tried to take him off guard. There was a sickening *crunch* as its head separated from its body and rolled down the hill.

"Shins, no!"

Midnight heard Polly's cry and instinctively ran back in her direction, leaving Gredge and Giles to deal with the rest of the undead hoard. He reached the centre of the circle where Laura was restraining Polly. Midnight heard the struggle before he saw it.

The big shaggy wolf-dog—for want of a better word—was pinned to the floor on its back, its rear legs scrabbling frantically at the underbelly of its foe, trying desperately to disembowel him. Shins's huge claws tore through cloth and flesh, causing Hemlock to screech in pain but not let go of the massive jaws on which both his hands were clamped in an effort to rip off the animal's lower mandible. A whine of pain escaped from the 'dog's' throat, which Polly mirrored.

Midnight aimed his pistol at the pair but hesitated. The two forms were a roiling mass of limbs and fur. He could not risk accidentally shooting the animal. Once again, he opened himself to shadow and light. Usually, there were limits as to how much and how long he could use and hold the power inside of him without feeling drained but here, in this mystical place, he felt invigorated. A great plume of billowing smoke shot from his palm, merging with tendrils of luminescence to form a long, serpentine mass of concentrated energy. Midnight aimed for Hemlock's feet, forcing the energy to loop around the blackguard's ankles. He yanked him skywards, dangling him like a fish on a hook.

Now freed, Shins wasted little time recovering. The creature was on his prey in a flash. With a ferocious snarl, it sank its fangs into the soft tissues of Hemlock's neck and ragged him with merciless intent. Polly screamed and buried her face in Laura's skirts. The sucking sound of torn flesh and breaking bone was one Midnight would never forget, neither was the sight of his enemy's half-severed head dangling from bloodied shreds of sinew. Shins sat back on his haunches, his snout wet with sticky blood and tissue, panting in exhaustion but triumphant in victory.

"They're dead! Again."

Midnight looked to Gredge who had made the call. All of the undead were now laying in a great tangle of limbs and gore, unmoving. Their fight had ended the moment Hemlock's had.

"So is Nightingale," Midnight called back.

"You sure, this time?"

"See for yourself."

Midnight allowed himself a deep, cleansing breath of relief. It was really over. Eighteen months of looking over his shoulder, worrying about Polly's safety, was finally over. He reached for the girl, his hand smoothing the back of her hair, her face still buried in the folds of Laura's dress.

"Sweetheart, are you all right? Come here." Bending, he scooped her up and hugged her tightly to him.

"I'm fine. Don't squeeze so 'ard. Shins took care of me and Laura."

"Miss Carter. Where have you both been? And what are you doing here? Charlie said you'd been hurt, and then you were missing. I—"

"It's a very, very long story, sir. And we're both fine. If you please, if it's really done wiv, can we just go 'ome?"

"Not quite done with, I'm afraid," Gredge said, looking around at the carnage. "What are we going to do with this lot?"

24

RISKY BUSINESS

Inspector Anderson had taken some convincing. Grave-robbing devil worshippers performing satanic rituals in the middle of nowhere was not something he'd ever encountered before. When Gredge had finally persuaded him to come and look for himself, the expression on his face had been one of disgust mixed with total disbelief—not over the fact that Gredge's and Midnight's reports had been true, but that something as large-scale as this 'Devil's den', as he'd called it, could happen right under his nose without him knowing anything about it.

"So, you see, Inspector Anderson," Gredge explained, "Ms. Adams had been seduced by the sect leader, whoever this was." He booted the corpse of Hemlock Nightingale. "She orchestrated the kidnapping of both Lord Gunn's daughter and his housemaid upon the swine's instruction, making up the poisoning story to cover her tracks. Only her plan fell through when Miss Carter escaped with the girl. The sect had intended to sacrifice them both at the stones. Lord Gunn is somewhat of an expert of the occult. He believes the fresh corpses... er, and the not so fresh ones," he muttered, "were to be used as proof, if you like, of the members' commitment to the sect."

Anderson looked unconvincedly at Midnight, who continued with the explanation.

"Inspector Gredge is correct in his assumptions. One would assume the leader—" He, too, kicked Hemlock's corpse, "—would require evidence of the members' loyalty. What better way to prove one's commitment to their satanic cause than by robbing bodies from graves and morgues?"

"And the paw prints? Where do they fit in exactly?" Anderson probed.

"Ah! Your 'pack of rabid dogs', Inspector. You've heard of Burke and Hare, of course?" asked Midnight.

"Who hasnae?"

"I propose that the sect members were using trained fighting dogs to murder people and use their bodies as tribute."

"Hmpf," Anderson grunted, "because bodies in morgues and graveyards are so hard to come by, eh?"

"Well, no... but perhaps the perpetrators believed that murdering would place them in higher favour with their master? Who knows?" Midnight offered. He smiled, hoping that his and Gredge's cobbled-together fictitious explanation of events would be sufficient to placate Anderson.

The inspector scratched his chin, mulling things over in his mind. He watched as a team of his men loaded the bodies onto a cart. There was going to be a lot of paperwork on this one. He blew out a heavy breath. "I've got a lot more questions, and I still need to question Ms. Adams's staff, so dinae be going off back to London anytime soon, aye?"

"We'll be spending the rest of the summer at the cottage, Inspector. There's a legal matter I need to attend to and—" Midnight glanced towards the cart. "—a personal one, too."

"Aye. I'm sorry for your loss, Lord Gunn. Must be a shock, finding oot."

"The worst."

"Coincidence that Ms. Adams should join a bunch o' murdering Satanists during your visit, and it be your daughter and housemaid she conspired to kidnap, don't you think?"

Midnight kept his cool. "Not really. My cousin confided to me that she was in debt and planned to marry well in the near future. I think she may have had me in mind as her future spouse. Indeed, I did consider the idea at one point but realised my loyalties lay elsewhere. I fear my cousin may have taken my inadvertent rebuff rather too personally and subsequently fell under the spell of another." He kicked Hemlock one more time for good measure. "As I said in my statement, she had journeyed to meet a suitor in Edinburgh the night she went missing."

"Aye, you did." Anderson flicked through his notebook. "Lucky escape for you then, I suppose," he said grimly.

"Indeed. A Lucky escape for us all this night. If there's nothing else, I should rather like to get back home and check on my household?"

Anderson shrugged and nodded. "You can go, but no' far mind you. I've no' finished taking all of your statements yet."

"I'm sure Inspector Gredge can help fill in the details. See you back at the cottage for dinner," Midnight said to a tired-looking Gredge and winked. He tipped an imaginary hat at Anderson and left them to finish up. He had his own business to deal with.

Of course, it hadn't gone down like that at all. The actual explanation was so far beyond the realms of normality that bending the truth had been their only viable option. They couldn't very well tell Anderson about the real chain of events leading to the heap of bodies on the hill. He would've carted them all off to the asylum without a thought or had them hanged for murder. Poor Felicity, she really had been a victim in all of this. What he'd told Anderson regarding her part in it was mostly truth. She had been seduced by Hemlock. It'd been him that she'd intended to meet in the city, but then he'd murdered her, reanimated her fresh corpse—how, Midnight still did not understand—made her his puppet and sent her home with a mission to complete. The reasons for his cousin's involvement in this whole terrifying turn of events had, until a few hours ago, evaded him. Until Polly had instructed him to look into the mind of the Barghest she'd named 'Shins'. Looking into any animal's thoughts and memories was tasking. Animals didn't think the same way as humans, and they had their own 'language' which made the images even harder to interpret, but he indulged his daughter. In point of fact, Polly seemed quite taken with the creature, quite a worrying thought by anyone's standards.

As he made his way back to Samoch, he recalled placing his hands on the big shaggy head and what he'd seen when Shins had let him in.

It was dark, and there were trees and stones, not the monoliths but headstones... a graveyard. And a man. Hemlock. 'Bad smell. Death. Danger. Intruder. Watch' had been the essence of what he gleaned from Shins' memories. Viewed through its eyes, the memories came in thoughts and feelings rather than words.

Next Midnight was back in the dark, rainy alley near Edinburgh Waverley where he'd encountered the creature on their first night in the city. *Bad smell. Wrong. End it. It must die.*

He stared into the face of the dead lawyer, Mr. Rosemont, whose ashen face and milky eyes crinkled with murderous intent. He tasted flesh as teeth sank into the reanimated corpse, tearing and clawing until the body stopped moving.

The memory had skipped forward to its first encounter with Polly in the woods. *Good smell. Cub. Alone. Protect.*

And then to when it had spotted him looking for Polly: *Intruder. Strange. Powerful. Run!*

Shins had projected his memory forward again to the night of Ms. Adams coach accident. *Evil! Danger. Bad smell. Fight. Kill.*

So, *Midnight had thought*, it was you who attacked the coach but only because that bastard Hemlock was inside already pouring his poisonous plan into the innocent mind of his freshly murdered and reanimated cousin!

He saw Felicity and Hemlock being flung from the ruined carriage, Shins ready to pounce, but he smelled the scent of the girl cub on her and hesitated just enough to allow her to jump on a horse and gallop away. He turned to face down Hemlock who was holding something in his hand and muttering. A second later and there was a loud CRACK! A Pooka appeared. Hemlock clambered on its back, leaving Shins unsure of how to act—he would not attack a fellow Fae. Then he saw images of himself, facing Shins during the search for Felicity, heard himself say the words 'Hello beastie'. *Strange. Powerful. Good smell? Pack? Cub?* It seemed that Shins had recognised Polly's scent on him and identified them as part of the same pack.

"At least I know why you didn't eat me," he had muttered.

Shins had chuffed.

Midnight had refocused his efforts, skipping through the animal's memories and piecing together the puzzle. How he understood it was that Hemlock had either followed, or preceded him to Scotland and had begun experimenting with corpses robbed from neglected graves initially. When he was sure he had perfected whatever spell he'd managed to get his hands on, he'd begun targeting specific people relevant to his plans. Shins could not tell him how Hemlock had reanimated the dead or how exactly he'd been able to recruit the three Pooka to lure him away. Midnight would have to question the three goblin men who were presumably happily tending to the grounds at St. Francis hospital this very moment.

Something to look forward to, he had thought.

"So then, Widdershins. It appears I mistook you for the villain when you were in fact the hero of the hour."

Shins whined.

"My sincerest apologies."

"Did he tell you, Papa?" Polly had asked.

"To a point, yes. There's still a lot that I don't understand, but I don't suppose it matters now. Nightingale won't be bothering us anymore."

"He won't, but what about the others?"

"Others?"

"Shins told me many would be lookin' for us now they saw us."

The skin on his neck prickled, he was almost afraid to ask. *"Who saw us?"*

"Them." Polly pointed directly at the gap between the two giant volcanic rock columns. *"Shins says we need protecting. They saw us when you opened the door in the stones."*

"Shins says a lot for a dog."

A low growl rumbled in the animal's throat.

"He says he's not a dog, he's a Barghest. And you should be grateful he took care of me and Laura in the woods."

"You can talk to him?"

"*Uh-huh. Well not talk with my mouth. I can hear him in me 'ead.*"

Midnight looked from Polly to the dog-wolf-thing who sat panting merrily with his tongue lolling from his open mouth, as if thoroughly enjoying this exchange.

"*He'd like to stay with us, for a while anyway, to protect us. Can he, Papa? Oh, please say yes?*"

"*Do I have a choice?*"

Widdershins chuffed at him.

"*I suppose that answers that question.*"

Polly beamed. Nothing seemed to phase her. After everything she'd been through, she still found something to smile about.

"*Laura will be so 'appy. She likes Shins too. I'll go tell her.*" And off she ran to where Laura had been attending to a nasty wound on Giles's hand.

"*Does she indeed.*" Midnight eyed Shins. "*I hope you're housetrained.*"

The new family pet pinned him with an incredulous look and bared his teeth.

Midnight bared his own. "*I bite too. Remember that.*"

They regarded each other for a few moments, and an understanding passed between them.

"*It seems you and I have a lot to discuss. Are we really still in danger?*" Midnight felt a little silly talking to an animal as if it was a person, but Shins whined in response, clearly understanding the question. "*And do you know who 'they' are?*"

"*Woof!*"

"*Well, Shins, you had better disappear for the time being, we have an inspector to call. We can um... talk... later.*"

The animal had retreated into the woods whilst Gredge had sent word for the city police and Inspector Anderson to meet himself and Gunn at the stone circle.

LAURA, Giles and Polly had gone back to Samach Cottage some time ago where Midnight was sure they had been suitably fussed over, tended to, and fed within an inch of theirs lives by now. He was tired, hungry and in need of his family. And they *were* his family. Strange and quirky it may be, but it was his and ever-growing—he'd even acquired a dog born of the Otherworld for Christ's sake. But if Shins was right, and other threats would come, then he would tolerate having the shaggy mutt on his side, if only for Polly's sake.

But now his mind turned to other business, and this was the worst of it all: he had a funeral to organise.

EPILOGUE

"May the Lord bless you and watch over you. The Lord make his face shine upon you, and be merciful to you. May he look kindly on you and give you peace. In the name of the Father, and of the Son, and of the Holy Spirit, amen," said the priest, and he made the sign of the cross.

"Amen," chorused the small group of mourners that had gathered at the graveside of Ms. Felicity Adams.

"As we now commit her body to the ground, her final resting place, earth to earth, ashes to ashes, dust to dust, we commend her spirit to its new home. Eternal rest be granted to her and may the light everlasting shine upon her." The priest finished by throwing a handful of dirt into the hole where Felicity's coffin lay, which landed with a dull thud, and was punctuated by a doleful sob from Eunice Wick, Felicity's old cook.

One by one, the small party of people stepped forward to repeat the process that symbolised the committing of a body to the ground. Craigson went first, a surprisingly dispassionate look on his face, followed by the sobbing Mrs. Wick, and then a hobbling Bobby Mac aided by Midnight.

"Rest in peace, mistress," Bobby muttered, genuinely saddened by his employer's untimely passing.

Midnight patted him on the shoulder then reached down for a fistful of the freshly dug earth. He held on to it for a second, reflecting briefly at his cousin's demise and wondered, not for the first time, if he could've prevented it. The persistent feeling of guilt over her encounter with Hemlock and her subsequent death would plague him for a long time to come, of that he was sure. It was not her fault; it was his. He had failed to keep his cousin safe. He opened his hand and let the earth fall onto the lid of the mahogany coffin. "I am sorry," he said and stepped aside to allow the gravediggers to begin the burial.

Four mourners, that was all his cousin's life had amounted to. It was pitiful really.

The day before the funeral, Midnight had visited Glenhaven and had spoken to each of Felicity's staff in turn, handing them each an envelope containing a month's pay, from his own pocket, and a letter of reference. He was in talks with his solicitor over how to settle his cousin's estate and the debts she'd left behind. Felicity did have some family, although none had attended the funeral, and there was a will.

Midnight had decided to stay on at Samoch for the duration of the summer or at least until all of Ms. Adams legal affairs had been concluded, and the process of purchasing Cnoc Sithé was well under way. He also intended to find out more from Shins about who, or what, he had seen through the stone portal. The stones were close to the ruined castle and if he still intended to purchase it, he needed to be fully prepared. In the days following the extraordinary events atop that hill, Midnight had questioned the appropriateness of proceeding with such a purchase and if it hadn't been for Polly's insistence on the matter, he might have abandoned the idea entirely. According to Polly, Shins was in absolute favour of it, so it must be a good idea. Midnight had rolled his eyes and said, '*Ah! Well if the dog approves,*' which had earned him a growl from the shaggy creature.

There was to be no official wake, but Midnight gave Bobby Mac an envelope with some extra money in it and suggested that he, Craigson, and Mrs. Wick might like to go to the tavern and toast to their mistress.

Bobby shook his hand gratefully. "Much obliged, sir. Would you care to come wi' us for a dram?"

"Thank you, but no. I'm afraid I have some business to attend to."

"Aye, I suppose you do," Bobby said. "I wish you well then, sir." He paused then to clear his throat. "Will you find them a good home, the horses? I should hate for them to go to someone who doesn't appreciate them."

Midnight smiled at Bobby. "Actually, I rather thought I might purchase one or two myself. I admit to having a certain liking for Samson, and my cousin's horse I think may do as a mount for my daughter. She's expressed an interest in learning to ride, God help me."

Bobby Mac whistled. "Well, sir, good luck wi' Samson. I dinnae envy you that responsibility. But the mistress's horse is a good choice for the wee bairn. She'll serve you well. I'm glad. And I know you'll see the others right too. Thank you." He nodded at Midnight. "And no' just for the horses, for the physician too. I appreciate it very much."

"It was my pleasure. I wish you well, Mr. MacDonald."

Bobby, Craigson, and Wick left Midnight alone in the graveyard. The bright summer sun seemed at odds with the melancholy of the occasion. There was a bench nearby, situated under the gently swaying branches of a willow tree. He went to sit on it, feeling obligated to stay until the last shovel of earth had covered Felicity's coffin- she shouldn't be alone. Midnight lowered himself on to the seat, removed his hat, closed his eyes, and turned his face skyward. The heat of the sun still reached him through the shade of the rippling branches although it did nothing to warm his soul.

The cold lump of dread in the pit of his stomach returned in his solitude and his eyes flicked open. A gentle breeze whispered amongst the leaves of the weeping willow, echoing the long expulsion of breath he forced through pursed lips in an effort to settle his sudden and inexplicable feeling of vulnerability. He had always felt comfortable in his own company, craved it even, and yet now he was experiencing something rather unfamiliar... he was lonely.

As he sat there, watching the dappled sunlight dancing playfully on the green grass at his feet and over the stark stone grave markers dotted around the churchyard, he thought of Ms. Adams and the pitiful funeral attendance and wondered who would show up to his own service. It had not occurred to him before that the lack of people might reflect such a lonely and isolated existence. If indeed he did live to a ripe old age—not likely given his circumstances—who would be left to bid him farewell?

Giles and Mrs. P. were much older than him. Charlie and Laura may still be in his employ by then but who could say, perhaps they would eventually marry and leave. And he wouldn't blame them if they did since being in his employ had almost cost them both their lives. That left Polly. He pictured his daughter grown, a solitary figure standing by his graveside, possibly the only person to mourn his passing. It was not a comforting prospect at all. His mind wandered to Miss Carter and the cold, heavy lump in his stomach shifted to a warm, excited flutter tainted with confusion and shame.

How long would she stay at Meriton after what had passed between them? In the days following the battle on the hill, things had been somewhat strained between them, and he wasn't sure how to fix it. Midnight sighed again and scrubbed a hand over his face.

He was about to stand up and leave when he noticed a familiar figure enter the churchyard and approach the site where two men were still hard at work filling in Ms. Adams grave. Midnight grabbed his hat, stood up and called, "Arthur?"

Inspector Gredge turned and scanned the yard.

Midnight stepped out from the shade of the tree and Gredge hurried towards him. The cold lump returned as he noted the expression on his friend's still-bruised face. "What?" He demanded as Gredge reached him.

Arthur shook his head and looked at the ground.

"What is it? Tell me," Midnight insisted.

"I've just come from Anderson's office. Had to go over my report again. Took some bloody explaining all this shit." Gredge waved his arm in the general direction of Ms. Adams' grave. "Anderson's like a bleedin' bloodhound. Doesn't give up. I still don't think he's fully convinced."

"Arthur!" Midnight grabbed Gredge by the shoulder.

"I'm getting there! Listen, this is what I'm trying to tell you. It's not over, Midnight. Anderson isn't convinced because... because—"

Midnight felt a chill run down his spine as he watched his friend grapple with his words.

"He's gone. Hemlock's body is missing from the bloody morgue!"

ACKNOWLEDGMENTS

Huge thanks must go to my readers, who have stuck with me and waited patiently to be reunited with Midnight & Co. I truly hope you enjoy this next instalment. I must also applaud my fellow 'Black Foxes' Lorna, Laura, and Nigel for their support, friendship, and hard work in helping my beastie take form. A note of thanks to the amazing Helen Taylor, whose vocal performances in THE HOLLOWS audiobook entertained my listeners so wonderfully, and whose generosity has warmed my soul. I look forward to your narration of THE BARGHEST. A nod to those wonderful betas who rescued my story from my own impatience. A special thank you to Bridgette for the wonderful new covers.

Finally, my wonderful, long-suffering, family for putting up with me during Barghest's creation. I love you beyond measure.

ABOUT THE AUTHOR

C. L. Monaghan is a self-confessed Scotophile living in the Kingdom of Fife. Writer of award-winning Gothic and historical mystery, and paranormal romance. Lover of hairy coos and red squirrels. Explorer of ancient ruined castles and beautiful glens. You can discover more about her and her books at: www.clmonaghan.com

 facebook.com/Joesbookbar

twitter.com/MonaghanAuthor

 instagram.com/clairemonaghan73

ALSO BY C. L. MONAGHAN

The Immaginario Duet

Immaginario

Andato

The Midnight Gunn Series

The Hollows

The Barghest

OTHER WORKS FROM HUDSON INDIE INK

Paranormal Romance/Urban Fantasy

Stephanie Hudson

Sloane Murphy

Xen Randell

Sci-fi/Fantasy

Brandon Ellis

Devin Hanson

Crime/Action

Blake Hudson

Mike Gomes

Contemporary Romance

Gemma Weir

Elodie Colt